MW00583532

THIS
IS
Love

THIS
IS
Love

IVY SMOAK

This book is a work of fiction. Names, characters, places, and incidents are fictitious. Any resemblance to actual persons, living or dead, events, or locales is purely coincidental.

Copyright © 2019 by Ivy Smoak
All rights reserved

ISBN: 9781942381136

Cover art copyright © 2020 by Ivy Smoak

2020 Hardcover Edition

To Ryan. You're the only reason I know how to write about love. This series exists because of you. Even if you are #TeamTyler.

PART 1

CHAPTER 1

Monday - *James*

I had forgotten how much I craved Penny's touch until I couldn't have it. That's what time did. Made perfection feel like normalcy. But it was easy to remember just how lucky I was when the one thing I craved was stripped from me. And I'd never take her for granted again. I'd never lose my temper. I'd never put my own needs first. I'd treat her the way she deserved.

Because Penny was everything to me. The sun rose and set with her. She was the air I breathed. She was the only vice I needed. And relying on a person was so much better than relying on any substance. I was okay with this bleak feeling of existence if I knew she was coming back to me. And I knew I was close.

When I had left the apartment tonight, her eyes were begging me to stay. She had been waiting for a kiss. And as much as I wanted to close the distance, I knew that I needed her to lean the rest of the way in. Me pushing her hadn't helped. Me trying to manipulate the situation had helped even less. She needed to make the decision to stay. To try and remember us. And she would. She had to.

In the meantime, holding my son was comforting. He was a little piece of her. A piece of her that wanted me, was relying on me, loved me. I watched his chest rise and fall without the machines and breathed a little easier myself. "Your mom's going to remember."

He squirmed in my arms.

I smiled down at him. "And we're going to take you home soon." I said those words almost every time I saw him. I didn't know if they were true. But I felt like if I kept saying it, then it would miraculously happen. I couldn't lose my son. I just couldn't.

"What do you want to do tonight?" I asked him. Every night, I'd hold him until visiting hours were over. Just the two of us. And I was very aware of the fact that it should have been three. But he was a pretty good distraction. Especially his blue irises. It almost felt like I was looking into Penny's eyes. Like I was close to her even though actually being this close to her freaked her out right now. A minor setback.

Earlier tonight I was almost positive that she had been waiting for me to kiss her. It was all over her face. I was holding out hope that part of the reason she wanted a kiss was that she was starting to remember. And even if she didn't remember, it was still a good sign. It meant she wanted me regardless.

After Penny read the book she wrote, she'd definitely be swayed the rest of the way. She was reading right now, trying to remember our love story. She'd look at me differently when I got home later. Hopefully she'd look at me with love in her eyes instead of unfamiliarity and fear.

"How about we look up the movie she apparently loves so much." I placed Liam down on my lap and pulled my phone out of my pocket. I leaned down and showed him the screen, even though I knew he couldn't read the Wikipedia article I had brought up about The Princess Bride. "A romantic comedy," I said. "It figures." I looked back down at my son. "She loves them. You'll see when you're older and she makes us all watch them with her."

I looked back at the screen. The article mentioned the phrase "as you wish" several times. It was exactly what Penny had talked about. But each time I saw it, the words felt more familiar. "Where have I heard that before? Do you know?"

My son blinked at me.

"Yeah. I don't remember either. Now we know how your mom feels."

He blinked again.

"As you wish," I said. "As you wish." I slid my phone back into my pocket and lifted Liam into my arms. "As you wish."

I could have sworn he sighed, like he was tired of my obsession with the phrase.

"And why wouldn't she have mentioned it to me if it was her favorite movie?" I began to rock Liam in my arms. "As you wish." All I could recall was a Disney song about wishing on a star. "Maybe I've just seen the movie before. We could watch a little of it right now if you want. How does that sound?" I smiled at him. "I know I'm not technically supposed to use my phone in here, but it can be our little secret." I pulled my phone back out and adjusted Liam in my arms so we could both see the screen. "This is your mom's favorite movie," I whispered right before it began. "We're going to surprise her by knowing all about it." I kissed the top of Liam's head.

But my smile almost immediately faded. "Is it me, or does Westley look a lot like Tyler?"

I frowned and it looked like Liam frowned back at me.

"Don't make that face, little dude."

He continued to frown at me, which made me laugh. "Cut it out. I'm sure it's just a coincidence. Your mom's having trouble remembering, but she loves me with all her heart and..." my voice trailed off. *As you wish.* The familiarity of the phrase came back in a rush as soon as Westley said it in the movie. "Oh fuck." I immediately dropped my phone in order to cover Liam's ears. "Sorry. Sorry." I pulled my hands away from his ears. "You won't remember that, right? Let's just pretend it never happened. It can be our little secret." I leaned down to lift my phone off the ground as I swallowed down another curse in my throat. Penny had a keychain with those words etched into it beside a metal heart. A keychain that Tyler had given her. That she had kept all these years. I looked back down at the image of Westley on the screen. They really did look similar.

I tried to shake away the thought. They didn't look *that* similar. And the keychain was just a gift. But my optimism still felt squashed. I tried to picture her closing her eyes, waiting for my kiss earlier this evening. It was harder when it felt like she was waiting for Tyler's. Her never mentioning the movie to me confirmed all my suspicions. Why would she tell me it was her favorite if it reminded her of another man?

Liam squirmed in my arms.

"You know, you're probably right," I said. "She used to like it and now she doesn't. Besides, she doesn't remember Tyler either. And you should have seen her after I mentioned the song we danced to at our wedding. She remembered. I could see it on her face. She's remembering me." I ran my hand along the side of his small cheek. "She's remembering us. And she'll remember that Tyler is just a friend."

But what if her memories didn't all come back at once? What if she started to remember from the beginning when she liked both Tyler and me? Like in her manuscript I had just given her to read...

"You know what, little dude? I need to cut out a little early tonight. I know, I know." I leaned down and kissed his forehead.

"When our family is put back together again you'll be thanking me. I need to go pull a grand romantic gesture to keep her attention on us."

I stared at him squirming in my arms. "I know she doesn't always like grand gestures, but she'll like this one." I had been carrying her engagement ring around in my pocket for days. I wanted to give it back to her, but something had been stopping me. It felt like I needed to ask her again. I was going to get down on one knee and ask her to choose me. I needed to hear her say I was what she wanted. And I wanted her to know how much I loved her too.

I knew it was just a movie. Just a keychain. Maybe it meant something in the past, but it didn't now. The Penny I knew didn't seem to like this movie anymore. She definitely didn't mention it because it was no longer her favorite, not because she was hiding some deep love for Tyler. Now I just needed her to remember.

The doctors had told me to take it slow. To ease her back into her life. But slow was killing me. Nothing Penny and I did had ever been slow. "I'm going to go win your mother back once and for all."

Liam just stared at me.

"It's not a bad idea. You'll see, little dude."

He had no reaction.

"I promise I'm thinking straight despite the fact that I'm exhausted." As if on cue, I yawned. "I'm not even that tired," I said through another yawn. I motioned for the nurse in the hall to come put him back in his incubator. "Next time I see you, I'll be whole again. And your mom's going to remember you. And we'll be one big happy family." I pulled him close to my chest. *Please don't make me a liar, Penny. Please remember.*

I took a deep breath, wishing my lungs could do the work for Liam's weak ones. "I love you." I kissed the side of his forehead. "I'll be back in the morning. Keep breathing for us." But really I meant keep breathing for me. Because if his little heart stopped, I was afraid mine would too.

CHAPTER 2
Monday - *James*

I wanted to be able to propose the same way I had the first time around. But I couldn't leave New York again. Liam and Scarlett needed me here. I just had to think of something similar to me popping the question in the coffee shop.

Penny didn't remember our favorite pizza place here in the city. Or where we had our wedding. Or where we danced in Central Park under the stars. She didn't remember anything here and had only really spent time in our apartment. An apartment proposal didn't feel romantic enough.

Maybe Liam was right. Maybe this was a bad idea. I almost laughed out loud. Liam hadn't said anything. The whole conversation we'd shared had just been me talking to myself. But I liked bouncing ideas off of him. The NICU was the one place where it felt like I could be open with everything I was thinking. As long as one of the nurses wasn't in the room.

I shoved my hands into my pockets and felt the ring. I should have just given it back to her when she woke up. But I saw the way she looked down at the tan lines on her ring finger. She looked appalled. *The same way she looked at me.*

I was trying to be strong for her. But I wasn't sure how much more I could take without breaking down. She didn't realize how important she was. Liam and Scarlett needed her just as much as I did. *Scarlett.* I needed to talk to her again. If she kept saying stuff like Penny wasn't her mom, Penny would feel like she truly wasn't. I needed Scarlett to believe that Penny was coming back as much as I believed it. I just hoped that the idea of Penny remembering didn't turn out to be a figment of my imagination. Lying to myself was one thing. Lying to my daughter was another. I tried to focus on the ring in my pocket again instead of my dismal reality.

I sighed. It didn't have to be a grand proposal. I'd just ask Penny if she'd do me the honor of wearing the ring again. Of taking a leap of faith on her family.

The fresh air made it a little easier to breathe. And the image of Penny closing her eyes and waiting for a kiss came back to me. She wanted me. And she was reading the beginning of our love story all night. She'd want me more when I got back than she did when I'd left.

I took a deep breath and stopped in front of the doors of our apartment building. I wanted to walk back into our apartment and see her face light up like it always used to. I wanted her to run over to me and throw her arms around the back of my neck as I pulled her in for a kiss. I wanted my life back.

I closed my eyes and prayed to a God I wasn't sure if I believed in. *Please let everything go back to normal. Please let her remember.* I promised to be a better man for her. A better father to my children. I wouldn't get lost in work. I'd be present and listen to what they wanted instead of assuming what they must want.

Penny asked for space while she remembered. I opened my eyes. It was true, she had asked for space. But she didn't look at me like she wanted space. She stared at me like she wanted anything but space between us. And even though I wanted to respect her boundaries, I wasn't sure if she was being true to herself either.

I opened the door and stepped inside. That was the whole problem. I did what I thought was best instead of listening. The unsigned contract that was locked in my desk drawer was a good sign of that. I had gotten her a publishing deal when she had specifically asked me not to. If I had just listened to her, I would have been here when she went into labor. I would have been here when she needed me.

I stepped onto the elevator. I should have taken the stairs. The extra exercise would do me good. My heart was feeling stronger every day despite the fact that it was broken. But Liam was right, I was tired. I almost laughed out loud again at the thought of Liam saying that to me. I desperately needed rest. I needed to sleep on the idea of proposing before I scared Penny further away. That was my biggest fear. That she'd leave again. That this time she'd never come back. I couldn't let that happen.

Tonight I'd sleep in the guest room. I wouldn't touch her. I'd do everything she'd asked unless she specifically said she changed her mind. Only then would I invade her space. I stepped off the elevator and put my key into the lock. *Please ask me, Penny. Let me back into your life.*

I didn't expect her to come running into my arms like she used to. But the house was eerily quiet. I walked into the kitchen, then the dining room, then the living room. The pages of her manuscript were all over the coffee table, but she was nowhere in sight. "Penny?" I called.

Melissa walked into the living room. "She went for a walk. And keep your voice down, Scarlett's asleep."

"You let Penny go for a walk alone?"

"No. Chill for two seconds. She went with one of the security guards. How incompetent do you think I am?"

"I didn't say that you were..."

"You kinda implied it." She plopped down on the couch. "I feel like you and I need to have a talk."

"Melissa, I wasn't calling you incompetent."

"Not about that." She waved her hand through the air, dismissing the altercation. "We need to talk about Penny. And you. And whatever game it is you're trying to play with her head. I made a few phone calls and read some articles and I'm pretty sure you're not supposed to be force feeding her the past." She nodded to the manuscript. "You're supposed to let her remember on her own time."

"She asked to read it."

"Fair enough, but you could have postponed it. I know you want her to remember. We all do. And I get that she's not just your wife. She's your best friend. Your confidant. And right now you can't confide in her so…confide in me. It might alleviate some of your stress."

"Melissa, I have people I can confide in."

"Who? Rob?" She laughed. "Trust me, he's about as good at pillow talk as a brick wall."

"Maybe with you."

She glared at me. "Has anyone ever told you that you're a terrible host?"

"Has anyone ever told you that you're a terrible house guest?"

She laughed. "I feel like I'm a normal house guest. There is no such thing as a good house guest. That's why you usually put everyone up in hotels, right?"

"It's more of a privacy thing."

"I see. Tell me more about that."

"I'm not going to talk to you about my issues."

"Why not?"

"Because you'll tell Penny everything I say."

"I can keep a secret, James. If you recall, it wasn't my fault your affair with a student leaked. I feel like I've earned your trust. And right now, you need to vent. I mean...you look like hell. Have you even been sleeping?"

"Melissa..."

"If you're not going to talk to me, you should talk to someone. I'm pretty sure Penny fell in love with the sweeter side of you. Not whatever this is." She gestured to me.

It was hard not to be a little offended.

"I mean, you do want her to fall in love with you again, right? New memories of you might kind of outweigh the old ones." She glanced back at the manuscript pages. "Huh. You might already be scaring her away. She wasn't even reading about you." She lifted up one of the pages and started reading out loud:

We slowly swayed back and forth. This was probably the sweetest thing a guy had ever done for me. I moved closer to him so that our bodies were touching.

"So you like it nice and slow?" Tyler said gently.

"If you are referring to dancing? Yes, isn't this nice?"

He leaned down to kiss me. I wanted to forget about Austin and I needed to forget about Professor Hunter. I grabbed the back of his head and pulled him closer as he kissed me deeply. His hands slid down from my waist and grabbed my ass.

"Stop," I said. "I don't need to hear about Tyler's hands on my wife's ass, I've already read it." Hearing about Tyler right this second wasn't helping. I was already a little pissed off about Penny's favorite movie revolving around him.

"See. You're angry."

"Because you're reminding me that she used to have her hands all over someone else."

"Everyone has exes, James."

"Not ones that they don't remember passing on."

"Aha. The root of the problem. What, are you scared that she's going to go back to him? He's married, remember?"

"It wouldn't be the first time someone cheated on someone else. It happens all the time."

"Aha! So this goes back to your first wife cheating on you."

"Would you stop saying 'aha' like this is actually a break-through?"

"Then just talk to me..."

"And say what? That I'm scared Penny will never remember? That I'm scared I'll have to go through the rest of my life in this fucking terrible numb state? That I'm worried I'm going to lose my son too? That when I think about everything I can't breathe?"

She stood up and hugged me.

I hadn't expected her to do that. For a moment, I stayed still, hoping she'd just let go. But when I finally forced myself to hug her back, I felt a sense of relief. When was the last time someone had tried to comfort me? That wasn't fair. Tons of people had tried to comfort me when Penny was unconscious. But I had pushed them all away. Because that's what I did. I couldn't lie though, it felt really nice to be hugged.

"That's a good start," Melissa said and smiled up at me. "Tell her those things. Be real instead of suave."

"Trust me, I haven't been suave."

"You're always suave. It's kinda your thing."

I laughed.

"Oh my God, did I just get you to smile?" She leaned closer. "Yup, you're officially smiling. See...doesn't it help to talk?"

I sighed, but it was just for show. "Sure."

"This is what girls do," she said and sat back down on the couch. "We talk everything out. So pretend you're a girl for a few minutes and chat with me." She patted the couch beside her.

"This is a ridiculous exercise." But for some reason, I found myself sitting down.

"So you said you were scared she'll never remember. Let's say the worst happens and she never does. What then?"

"Then...nothing. There is no me without her."

"You're being a little dramatic, James. Good job, you're really finding your inner woman for this chat."

I wasn't being dramatic. I was serious. If Penny never remembered me, my life was over. I couldn't keep going without her. I thought of Scarlett upstairs sleeping peacefully and of my son attached to all those machines. If I gave up, I'd be letting them down. I knew that and yet...how could I keep going?

"But really," she said. "What would you do?"

I ran my hand down my face as I leaned back on the couch. "I don't know, Melissa. Does Penny leave me in this scenario?"

"Yeah, I'm talking worst case. She doesn't remember and skips town again because she can't stand you. What's your plan?"

"This isn't helping."

"I just want you to think about the absolute worst thing. And then we figure out how to make that not happen. Trust me, it's therapeutic."

I looked down at my lap. "Worst case?" I exhaled slowly. "Penny leaves and I spiral into depression. I start taking drugs again. I ignore my kids because they look like her. I shut everyone in my life out. And I probably overdose and die."

"Jesus that's dark."

I looked up at her. "You said worst case."

She laughed. "Yeah, I thought you'd say like…try to better yourself and win her back."

"I assumed in the worst case I couldn't win her back."

"Fair enough, drama queen." She laughed as she pulled her knees into her chest. "Okay, here's how to prevent doomsday. You know Penny better at 26 years old. But no one knows Penny better at 19 than I do. She desperately wants someone to love her for her. I think you loving her already makes her feel like you didn't get to know her. You know?"

"I guess?"

Melissa laughed. "You need to ask her more questions. Even if you already know the answers. Take interest in what she's saying. Maybe even pretend you don't know the answers. Make her feel…seen."

"Seen?"

"Yeah. After you two met, she told me that it felt like you saw her. I know…super cheesy. But it's what she said."

"I never knew that." I could picture Penny telling Melissa all about how we met. She hadn't gone into specific details in her novel. "What else did she say?"

"Well, she didn't take off the sweater you loaned her for hours. She kept talking about how good you smelled."

I smiled.

"Another smile? I'm on a streak," she said.

I thought about the engagement ring in my pocket. "So getting down on one knee and asking her to be my wife again is a bad idea."

"Yes. Wait, were you planning on doing that? It's too soon, James."

"I only knew her for two months before I proposed the first time."

"Which was crazy. That was something a crazy person would do."

I laughed. "If I hadn't recently gone through a divorce, I probably would have done it sooner. She's it for me, Melissa. Dramatic or not, she is."

She gave me the saddest smile. "Then take my advice and go slowly this time around. Okay? You don't want to spook her. She's already run away once."

Yeah. Melissa and Liam agreed. No grand gestures. *At least not quite yet.* I glanced at the coffee table. The manuscript almost looked like it had been shuffled around. I picked up one of the sheets and scanned it.

"Exactly how many girls have you slept with, Tyler?"

He leaned forward. "I'm going to pass."

"You're not allowed to pass."

He stared at me.

"That many, huh?"

"Look, I know why you're asking. You want to know if I've been with anyone since I started talking to you."

"So...?"

"Penny..."

"Oh my God, Tyler. You're such a slut," I whispered.

He gave me a mischievous smile. "I'm just messing with you, Penny. No, I haven't slept with anyone this semester. And only three girls total. There, that's not so bad, right?"

"What is wrong with you?" I leaned across the table and lightly shoved his shoulder.

"You're fun to mess with. You're so gullible."

"Very funny." I shook my head at him.

"Besides, now I got a question answered without even having to ask it," he said.

"Oh, yeah? And what is that?"

"You like me."

I kept my mouth shut.

"You got so jealous. You should have seen your face, Penny."

The first page Melissa had lifted up had talked about Tyler's hand on my wife's ass. And this one was about Penny pretty much admitting that she had feelings for him too. I grabbed another paper off the coffee table.

He really was a sweet guy. "Tyler, I can't ask you to miss your party for this. Melissa made it seem like it was going to be lots of fun."

"Trust me, there is nothing I'd rather be doing." He handed me the disc. I looked down and saw that it was The Princess Bride.

"This is my favorite movie."

"Yeah. I'd be lying if I didn't confess that Melissa told me. But I already owned it, because I like it too." He smiled at me as he pulled the popcorn out of the microwave, then sat on the end of my bed.

I put the movie in and sat down next to him.

"Popcorn?" he asked and put the bag down between us.

"You're a really good friend, Tyler."

"Yeah I know." He laughed and put his arms behind his head and leaned against the wall.

"No seriously. I've never really had a guy friend that was genuinely nice just because he cared."

"Honestly, I'm just paying my dues." He winked at me. "But I like being friends with you too. And since we're just friends, I can do stuff like this and not get in trouble." He slid over and put his arm around my back.

"Is that right?"

"I'm just here to take care of you." *He tapped his shoulder that was closest to me.*

"So I guess since we're friends I'm supposed to rest my head on your shoulder?"

"Well, I mean if you want. I just had an itch. But I promise I won't read into it."

I leaned my head on his shoulder. In the movie, Westley was just saying goodbye to Buttercup so he could go off and find a fortune so that they could get married.

"I never understood why she was always so mean to him at first," *Tyler said.*

"Because she didn't realize that she loved him yet."

"Right," *Tyler said. He rested his head on top of mine.*

I almost crumpled the paper in my hand. It wasn't just the keychain he had given her that had made me think I knew about Tyler's link to The Princess Bride. I had read all about it. I had read about it and forgotten it. All the parts about Tyler in this book I had shoved aside. But a lot of them were about him. It wasn't just Penny and my love story. It was like a twisted love triangle. I had given her this book hoping she'd remember me. And it looked like all she had been doing was remembering him.

"Why does Penny like The Princess Bride?" I asked.

Melissa shrugged. "Something about true love. I don't know. I never understood the appeal."

"Does it have anything to do with Tyler?"

"No. She liked it before she met him. Although, he did dress up like Westley for Halloween for her."

"What? When?"

"When you two were on a break."

A break. I said I needed time. We weren't really on a break. But I couldn't fault Penny for pursuing Tyler during that time. *Yet, here I am seething.* Why? Because of some stupid film that meant nothing? But that was the problem. It meant something to her. And she never told me. Maybe she liked it before she met Tyler, but it was all intertwined now. They snuggled while they watched it. He dressed up as the main character for her. And he gave her that stupid fucking key chain. I grabbed another paper off the table as my head started to spin.

I listened to his slow, steady heartbeat. I could lay here forever in his embrace. I let my hand wander beneath his shirt and felt his abs. His body seemed to tense from my touch, which made his muscles even more pronounced. He was so sexy.

"Are you feeling any better?" Tyler whispered.

"What the fuck is this?" I stood up. "All the pages on top are about him."

"Who?" Melissa asked.

"Tyler."

She leaned forward. "Oh, yikes." I watched as she bit into her bottom lip. Her eyes scanned more of the pages. She crossed and uncrossed her legs. "I mean…it kind of looks like they were shuffled around or something? But yeah…most of them are about Tyler. Almost like she picked through the book…but why would she do that?" She made a weird face, a combination of a grimace and confusion.

"Where the hell did you say she was?"

"She went for a walk with one of your security guards."

"Which one?"

"I don't know. But would you calm down for one second. This is probably just some misunderstanding. I mean..." She shuffled the papers around with her hands. "It seriously looks like she was just...I don't know...tossing them around."

"Tossing them around?" *Give me a fucking break.* She had read about Tyler and wanted to read more. I pulled out my phone and clicked on Porter's name.

He answered in one ring. "Mr. Hunter."

"Where's Penny?"

"She's with Ian. She went for a walk and..."

I hung up the phone.

"James," Melissa said. "You need to take five and calm down. Whatever it is that's running through your head, it's probably wrong."

"Probably?"

"Yeah. Probably. I'm not going to lie and tell you I'm 100 percent certain she didn't want to read about Tyler. I can't read her freaking mind. Anymore anyway."

"Do you know something?"

"What?" She awkwardly blew a strand of hair out of her face. "I don't know what you're talking about."

"Melissa, you can't ask me to open up to you and then keep shit from me. Did she go see Tyler?"

"No. Oh my God. I didn't lie to you. She went for a walk. But if I'm being totally upfront, she maybe has kinda sorta mentioned that Tyler is exactly her type."

It felt like my heart stopped. I felt the familiar pain cross my chest. I'd been having these sharp, fleeting pains ever since my cardiac episode. "Tyler and I look nothing alike."

"I know that. You're very different. In like...every way."

"You think she likes him?"

"Of course not. But in her 19-year-old mind, before she met you, apparently she had a thing for guys with blonde hair and blue eyes."

"And you didn't think this was important for me to know?"

"I'm telling you now. And I thought I took care of it. I told her that he was married. I told her that you're her type. I told her everything I was supposed to. You're acting like I don't have your back here...but I do. I'm on your side, James."

I pictured Penny knocking on Tyler's door. And putting her head on his shoulder as they watched her favorite movie. And him squeezing her ass. And her hand groping his abs. "I'm going to kill him."

"She's not at Tyler's, James. She went for a walk."

I dialed Ian's number.

"I'm in the middle of a Jen emergency, James," Ian said when he finally answered. "If there's any way that this can wait until tomorrow..."

"Where the hell is Penny?"

The awkward silence stretched for too many seconds.

"Tell me right fucking now, Ian." Again, the pain seared across my chest. I'd been feeling it ever since my surgery, but I hoping it wasn't really related. I knew what having a cardiac episode felt like now. This? I was pretty sure my heart was breaking in two. It had been ever since Penny didn't wake up. Ever since she didn't recognize my face. Ever since our daughter had become a stranger to her. Ever since she didn't recognize Liam in her arms.

But this might be worse. It was all my worst fears coming true. Penny was finally waking up...to the fact that I wasn't the right choice all those years ago. I couldn't fix our lives if she left me. "Ian."

"I…" his voice trailed off. "She told me I could go. She said she was heading right back to the apartment." There was a shuffling of papers. "I'm so sorry, James. I'm heading back now, I…"

"It's fine. I know where she is."

"Oh. Geez. You nearly gave me a heart attack. I mean…" his voice trailed off and he awkwardly cleared his throat.

"It's fine," I said again, even though I didn't believe my own words. "I'll see you tomorrow."

"See you tomorrow."

I hung up the phone and slid it back into my pocket. "I'll be back in a bit. Could you keep an eye on Scarlett?" I tried to say it as cheerily as possible even though it felt like dark clouds were forming in my mind.

"Where are you going?"

I wasn't even sure why she asked. She knew exactly where I was going.

"Don't do anything stupid. She doesn't remember her life, James. You're holding her accountable and she doesn't remember. You need to cut her some slack."

Why, so that she'll leave me? I swallowed down the words instead of voicing them. There was no point in lying to Melissa. I was planning on pounding Tyler's face until he was unrecognizable. If he so much as laid a hand on her, he was dead.

CHAPTER 3

Monday - *James*

When I had stepped out of the hospital earlier today it felt like I could finally breathe again. But now? The night was hot and humid. It felt more like the buildings were caving in around me. Like the sidewalk was cracking under my feet. Like my whole world was being destroyed.

Here I was planning a fucking re-proposal and she was what? Sucking Tyler's cock?

A drop of rain hit the top of my head. I looked up to see the storm clouds above me through the darkened sky. Every time it rained, I thought of her. I always would. But she wouldn't be thinking about me. I tried to focus on putting one foot in front of the other.

Penny looked the same. She smelled the same. But she wasn't the same. Was this how people felt when their spouses died? Like their world was caving in around them? That's how I felt. Like the Penny I knew and loved was gone. Like she had been taken from me far too soon. And I couldn't get her back. No matter how hard I fucking tried to recreate our lives. Or show her that I cared. None of it mattered. Because one person caring in a relationship wasn't enough.

It started raining harder. Each drop felt like it seared my skin. I needed to stop before I did something I regretted. I needed to turn around and go back to my apartment. But my feet kept moving forward.

I didn't want to believe any of this was real. It was like Penny and I were on a broken wheel. Every time something went wrong in our relationship, she went back to Tyler. How many times could she run back to him before it stuck? How many times was she going to try to break me?

It felt like tears were running down my cheeks, but I couldn't really tell. It was pouring now. I was soaked from head to toe. I wished that I felt numb. I wished I never knew what it was like to feel this way. But if that was true, I never would have felt what it was like to be loved either. To love. I didn't know how to fucking live without her love.

My feet suddenly stopped. And I knew it wasn't rain on my cheeks. I broke down in the middle of a busy sidewalk in NYC and started crying. I felt my knees buckle and I fell to the ground and let myself cry. I let the grief of losing her overtake me. I let the feeling of hopeless take over.

I saw a dollar bill fall to the ground in front of me. Someone had mistaken me for a homeless person. A small act of compassion should have been able to improve my mood. But it didn't. It just made me feel worse. Because someone thinking I was homeless was fitting. The dollar bill blurred in front of me. Penny was home to me. And I had lost her. I had lost the only home I had ever really known.

In the blink of an eye the anger overshadowed the pain again. If Penny could remember Tyler, she could remember me. She was just choosing not to. Or something was blocking her. I needed her to see that I was the right choice. And showing up looking like a scraggly, wet homeless man wasn't going to help. I knew how she'd look at me. Like I was an addict. Like I was broken. Like she was scared of me.

When had I gotten used to her not recognizing me? When had that become more familiar than seeing her look at me with love in her eyes?

None of that mattered. Penny was the reason my heart kept beating. She was the reason that I could breathe. And I'd spend every second of the rest of my life trying to win her back. I needed to fix what I had broken. By breaking Tyler's nose. I knew it wasn't logical, but that's what motivated me to stand back up.

I didn't care that I was about to show up looking like a crazy man. And no matter what I was about to walk into, I'd forgive her. I'd forgive her and we'd move on. That was the only option. *She'll leave with me, right? She'll come back home. For me, for our kids.*

I pushed into the front lobby of Tyler's apartment complex and my anger only grew. I had helped him find this place. I had let him move two blocks away from me and my wife. I had been blind to what he was planning.

"Good evening, Mr. Hunter," said the woman standing in the reception area. "Are you…I mean do you…need a towel? Or…"

I ignored her and walked past the elevators and into the stairwell. Was that why Penny wanted Tyler? Because he was healthy? I'd be fine. I just needed to get back in shape. I walked up one flight of stairs before I had to stop on one of the landings.

Damn it! I slammed the side of my fist against the brick wall. She probably looked at me and saw weakness. My past. My present. I put my hand on my chest. I wasn't weak. I was healing. I just needed time.

I took another deep breath and forced myself up more stairs.

I'd prove to her that she wasn't better with Tyler. How had I not known she preferred guys with blonde hair and blue eyes? What was she, a fucking Nazi?

The thought actually made me laugh. The sound echoed around in the empty stairwell. *I'm losing my mind.* I buried my hands in my hair. *I've lost it.* I laughed again and then coughed as more tears threatened to escape.

Get a grip. I needed to win her back. But I wasn't opposed to dragging her back to our apartment caveman style. Penny was mine. She was mine. A piece of my heart was inside of her and she was just having trouble remembering. I'd remind her. I had to.

I almost slipped on the next landing from my wet shoes, but I pressed on. When I finally made it to Tyler's floor I was completely out of breath. But I knew if I stopped moving, I wouldn't be able to keep going. I'd stop. My heart would stop. Everything would stop.

I knocked on Tyler's apartment door. When no one answered after probably what was only a second, I knocked even louder. *You're dead, Tyler. Enjoy your last breaths.*

The door opened a moment later. But it wasn't Tyler standing there waiting for my wrath. It was Hailey. "Shh James, I just got Axel to bed." She held her index finger up to her lips like she was hushing a child. And then she laughed, like she knew she was talking to me like she did her son. She smiled up at me before concern crossed her face. "Is everything alright?" Her eyes scanned me, taking in my wet clothes, and maybe my red eyes.

Poor, sweet, naïve Hailey. She was in the same boat as me. She wouldn't be looking at me with pity when she found out her spouse was cheating on her too. I was going to fix this problem for both of us. I looked past her into their living room. "Where is he?"

"Who? Tyler or Axel?"

"Right, I'm here because I'm pissed off that your three-year-old son has a crush on my daughter. Yes Tyler." There was an edge in my voice. Probably because I was actually annoyed about the first thing I mentioned too. My daughter would never end up with a cheating, lying Stevens. We were done with this family. None of them would ever step foot in my home again.

She laughed. Like this was a time for laughing. "I knew you were upset about Axel and Scarlett having cute little crushes on each other. It's just a kid thing. I think it's adorable."

"Where is he?" I wasn't even listening to what she was saying. I walked past her and peered into their kitchen.

"I told you, I just put him to bed."

Jesus, this woman was driving me insane. "Not Axel. Tyler! Where is Tyler?"

"Would you keep your voice down? I had to read Axel three bedtime stories and…"

"Where the fuck is he?!"

She winced at my words. Or maybe it was just at my tone. I wasn't trying to direct my wrath at her, but she was standing in the way of what I wanted.

"Tyler isn't here. He's on a run," she said. "And I think you should go home, James. Whatever this is can wait until the morning. Don't you think?" That moment of weakness where she had winced was gone. She even seemed to be standing a little taller.

Couldn't she tell I was here to help her? "I'm not leaving until I speak to him."

She folded her arms across her chest. "I'm not going to ask you again. You need to go." Her bottom lip trembled slightly. I would have missed it if I hadn't been staring right at her.

She was scared of me. What the fuck was I doing? I swallowed down the lump in my throat. She needed to know the truth. She was tough, she could handle it. Probably better than I could. "He's cheating on you. He's with Penny."

"What?" She immediately unfolded her arms. "Why on earth would you think that?" She didn't believe me.

"Penny disappeared about an hour ago. She said she was going for a walk."

"So..."

"Right before that, she was reading the book she wrote. All the pages about Tyler were on top of the coffee table when I got home. She remembers him. She remembers him and she doesn't remember me." My voice broke. "She doesn't remember me, Hailey. She doesn't want to remember me. But Tyler? Apparently she wants to remember him."

Hailey's face softened. "She can't help how she remembers. Getting amnesia wasn't something she asked for."

"I've tried everything to jog her memory. Everything I could think of. And she reads a few pages about Tyler and runs to him?"

"You don't know that for sure."

"When did he leave to go on a run?"

She shrugged one shoulder. "About an hour ago."

See. Wasn't that proof enough? "Does he usually go on runs this late?"

She didn't look convinced of my theory at all. "No. He usually goes before work. But we were running late this morning. It's just a coincidence."

Was she blind? "They're together right now. We need to go find them. We need to stop them before Penny breaks your family apart too."

She drew her eyebrows together. "Tyler loved Penny in that way once. But he doesn't now. He's not stuck in the past like Penny is right now. Even if she makes a pass at him, he'll shut her down. He'll remind her that she loves you and only you. You're worrying about nothing."

"How are you so sure?"

"Because I know Tyler. I know him better than anyone in the world and he's not the kind of guy that cheats on his wife. Or steals someone else's wife, for that matter."

"He asked Penny to run away with him the day before our wedding."

"Oh, you mean the wedding that you called off? If you ask me, that was kind of on you. And he was in a bad place. He's been through so much. He was in pain and he was just trying to find comfort in the wrong place. Because he hadn't met me yet." She gave me a small, sad smile.

It was right after our wedding that Tyler and Hailey fell in love. Right after Penny rejected him. Couldn't she see that there was a hole in her logic? The only reason Tyler was with Hailey was because Penny had turned him down. She was his second choice. And right now, I wasn't Penny's any choice. She didn't even like me, let alone love me.

"Then call him," I said. "Prove me wrong."

"I will." She walked into the living room and picked her cell phone up off the coffee table. She pressed a few buttons and put her phone up to her ear. After several seconds ticked by, she pressed her lips together and looked down at the ground. Maybe a tiny bit of doubt was getting into her head. "He didn't pick up.

But he listens to music when he runs. He probably just has the call function turned off or whatever."

"That's not a thing."

"You don't know that."

"I'm a tech guy. I do know that. A cell phone's primary function is to you know…be a phone."

"God, you're such an old man. If anything, a cell phone's primary function is for texting. Well, that and watching cat videos on YouTube."

I glared at her.

She glared back.

"Then text him," I said.

"He can't run and text."

"You're making excuses for him. I'm telling you that he…"

"James, I've been patient with you. But I will not have you stand in my home and insult my husband. And insult me. I'm sorry that you're hurting. I'm sorry that Penny doesn't remember you. I can't even imagine what you're going through. If you'd like to talk about it, I'm here to listen. But if you say one more thing about Tyler I'm going to…punch you."

"You're going to punch me?" Was she serious? I just stared at her. All Stevenses were the worst. Even the ones that were married into the family.

"Yes. And it's going to hurt. I have a mean left hook." She held up her hand in perfect form. Most people who had never punched anyone would tuck their thumb underneath their other fingers. But she was doing it right. No thumbs would be broken if she decided to collide her fist into my jaw.

"My dad taught me how to defend myself. And I know to use words first, but you're testing my patience. So you best be getting ready for a beat down if you say one more thing about

Tyler." She made a fist with her other hand too and started moving them in the air in a gesture that could only be seen as playful.

I laughed. I couldn't help it. The thought of her attacking me was too humorous.

And she started laughing too.

"I'm sorry, James." She dropped her hands as she approached me. "Really, I can't imagine the hell that you're living. My heart aches for you." She threw her arms around me. And for the second time tonight, I let myself be hugged by someone who had never hugged me before.

Hailey knew what it was like to lose everything she loved. Her father died a few years ago. He was her only family. Tyler was there to catch her when she fell from that loss. And it was fucked up of me to think that he'd suddenly stop being there for her. Just because Penny thought she was a teenager, it didn't mean Tyler had suddenly forgotten the past several years. And he loved Hailey. I knew what love looked like. I used to have it. "I'm sorry."

"It's okay," she said into my chest. "I'm sorry I threatened to punch you."

I laughed. "It's okay."

She dropped her arms from around me. "Wait, James, what if Penny isn't with Tyler?"

I'd been so focused on her running to Tyler that I hadn't even thought of that possibility.

"If she's not with him, do you have any idea where she is? Let me try to call Tyler again."

Where is she? The words echoed around in my head. Jesus, why hadn't I even thought of that? Where the hell was my wife? "Call everyone we know. I'm gonna call the police."

She didn't tell me I was jumping to wild conclusions this time. She was on her phone faster than I was.

"Rob?" she said into her cell. "Is Penny there with you?" The brief pause seemed agonizingly long. She shook her head at me. "We think she's missing."

I had spent all this time thinking she was running back to Tyler. I had never even thought that there could be something worse. I never even considered the fact that there was a threat looming. Dr. Nelson was still out there. He had already tried to kill her once. And I wasn't with her to protect her. There was nothing to stop him from trying again.

PART 2

CHAPTER 4
Monday - *Penny*

There was a strange pressure building inside of my chest. It felt like I was about to cry. Why was I falling apart here? I had everything I wanted in this man. But what he had just done to me. The way he had made me feel. Now everything felt more real.

I quickly sat up and pulled my legs in, hugging them close. The tightness in my chest was growing. It felt like I was drowning. I took a deep breath to try to calm myself. What is wrong with me?

Professor Hunter sat up and cupped my chin in his hand. "Penny, what's wrong?" *His brow was furrowed.*

"Nothing." *I blinked to try and remove the tears that were trying to fall. I hugged my legs tighter.*

He rubbed the side of my chin with his thumb and didn't say a word. He looked truly concerned.

"It's just. For some reason, this whole time, it's seemed like I made this all up. Like it's this fantasy and you're not real. And I'm afraid that I'm going to wake up from this amazing dream and you're going to be gone. That you're just going to disappear."

"I've told you that I'm not going anywhere. There's no reason to be upset about that. Please don't cry." *He wiped away one of the tears that had fallen down my cheek.*

"But what we just did. I know you said you were going to be gentle. But I expected it to be like the other times. This whole day just seemed different. More intimate. I don't know. I didn't expect to feel so...so..."

"No one's ever made love to you."

I felt embarrassed. He didn't even ask it like it was a question. He just knew. Why had I opened my mouth? *"Well, I thought so. But no, not like...not like that."* I was so pathetic.

"I didn't mean to make you uncomfortable." He rubbed another tear off my cheek. *"How many partners have you been with?"*

Sexual partners? What the hell is this conversation? *"One."* I *felt so inadequate. If I wasn't uncomfortable before, I definitely was now.*

He wrapped his arms around me and pulled me down on top of him. I expected him to say something, but he just held me against his chest. I listened to his steady heartbeat.

I had a feeling that I didn't want to know the answer to my next question, but I couldn't resist asking anyway. "And how many partners have you been with?"

He sighed. "A little more than that."

"How many more?"

"Penny, I don't want to you to think poorly of me."

"More than five?"

He sighed again.

"More than ten?"

"I spent a large portion of my college years fairly drunk."

"More than fifteen?"

"We should probably stop playing this game."

"Professor Hunter, you're a slut!"

He laughed. "You seem to enjoy all my experience."

I cringed. I didn't like to picture him with other women.

"And what about your one, Penny?"

"What about him?" I didn't want to talk about Austin. Not at all, ever. *But especially not here in Professor Hunter's bed. I slid off of him onto my side and rested my head in my hand.*

"One is rather intimate. Is he someone I should be worried about?"

I laughed. "No."

"So you no longer speak to him?"

Did he somehow know that I had seen him this semester? "No. I doubt that I'll ever talk to him again. He's an immature asshole."

"And why is that?"

"Why do you want to know?" I didn't want to be talking about this.

"Because I don't want to make the same mistakes with you that he did."

I sighed. I wanted this conversation to be over. "There isn't much to tell. We dated last semester. He didn't speak to me all summer. He made me feel worthless."

"So you broke up with him?"

"You can't really break up with someone who you never officially went out with."

He took my hand in his. "Penny Taylor, I promise not to make you feel worthless. And I'll try not to act like an asshole." He smiled. His fingers intertwined with mine.

"I don't know, Professor Hunter. From what I've found out about you, it seems like I'm just going to end up as another notch on your bedpost."

He laughed. "That's not who I am anymore."

"I thought it was impossible for people to change?"

"I came here for a change. And I think I'm better off because of it." He pulled me toward him so that my head was resting on his chest again. I let my leg cross over him.

I felt so safe in his arms. I knew why I had gotten so upset tonight. Because I wasn't just fucking my professor. I was in deep. I loved him. I'm in love with my Comm professor. I breathed in his sweet scent. This moment could last forever and it wouldn't be long enough.

***

"Penny. Penny." He was lightly tapping the side of my face. "Penny, wake up. Please wake up."

I felt my smile stretch to meet his palm. I remembered. I remembered pieces at least. All the dreams I had been having, they weren't dreams at all. They were memories. Memories of us. The book I had written confirmed it. While I was reading, I could so clearly picture the scenes unfolding. I remembered. *I think.*

The side of my face felt wet, like I was crying tears of joy. I slowly opened my eyes. They felt heavy. It was as if my eyelids weighed a pound each. *Ouch, my head.* I lifted my hand and felt more wetness everywhere. *Rain. Oh, I do love the rain. I remember now. I remember!*

"Penny."

Rain was falling down on my face. I blinked as the man in front of me came into focus. It wasn't James. It was...Tyler? The dirty blonde hair. His crystal clear blue eyes. Who else could it be? "Tyler?" My voice came out hoarse.

"Oh, thank God." It looked like he was crying. But maybe it was just the rain on his face. He leaned down and hugged me.

The side of his neck felt hot against my cheek. My heart started racing. This was Tyler. *The Tyler.* The one I turned down to be with James? His arms felt nice around me. I took a deep breath and smiled. He smelled like grass and sunshine, even though it was raining. My head ached, like memories were trying to escape. Memories of him and me.

"Everything's okay, Penny. I've got you."

I was about to ask where we were, but when I looked up at Tyler I saw blood dripping down the side of his chin. There were splotches of it on his shirt. He was completely soaked from the rain, but it didn't wash away the blood.

"You're bleeding." I reached up and lightly touched the side of his jaw.

He flinched.

"Are you okay? What happened?"

"I'm fine," he used a soothing voice like he would with a child. "The police are on their way. You're safe."

I realized I was cradled in his arms. Like he was holding my body together, lest I fall apart and wash away in the rain.

Safe from what? There was a light flickering above us. And sirens wailing in the distance. It did not look like we were in a good part of town. There was a man standing next to a cab talking animatedly on his cell phone. He kept pointing to the left. I tilted my head and saw a body lying in a pile of black trash bags on the side of a curb.

It came back in a rush. The man claiming to be my father-in-law's friend. My memories were colliding. Scarlett was afraid of snakes. And I didn't just learn that from the zoo the other day. I knew it. I remembered! I remembered her before I was in the hospital! My sweet, baby girl. And she called them snapes instead of snakes. Like Professor Snape from Harry Potter. That man lying unconscious in the pile of garbage had looked just like Professor Snape. He had said I was supposed to die. That I was supposed to fix his life, not ruin it. "Dr. Nelson." My voice sounded weird. "Is that Dr. Nelson?"

"Don't worry," Tyler said. "He's unconscious and the police are on the way. Sayem called them." He nodded toward the cab driver.

"What happened? How'd we get here?" I shifted in his arms, but didn't push him away. Him being close to me was so comforting.

"I was on a run and saw that bastard shoving you into his car. I couldn't catch up but luckily I hailed down the world's best taxi driver. He broke all sorts of traffic laws tailing Dr. Nelson. Probably got caught by at least 10 traffic cameras. Think James could help him get out of a few tickets?" He smiled.

I was pretty sure he was making a joke about James, but I didn't laugh. "And you...knocked him out?" I asked. He saved me.

"I took him by surprise. I never would have let him hurt you."

I stared up at him. He was literally my knight in shining armor. The sharp angles of his jaw were worthy of a romance book cover. And his hair was wet from the rain but somehow still looked good. He was wearing a t-shirt and the rain made it cling sexily to the muscles in his chest. It felt like my heart was beating faster than humanly possible. I was aware of his hands on my body. His warm breath invading my air supply in a good way. "You saved me."

He pushed my hair out of my face. And I had the overwhelming sense that I wanted him to kiss me. I remembered the pages I had read about him from my book. I had liked him all those years ago. I knew that I had.

So how had I wound up here? With his arms wrapped around me in the most loving way, yet he had a wife and I had a husband? How cruel fate could be. How had the universe not seen that Tyler Stevens was my perfect match? After all, I did fit perfectly in his arms. "What happened to us?"

He looked down at me with his beautiful blue eyes. "Everything that was supposed to."

"I feel closer to you than I do to James. Why is that? He's cold and ill-tempered and you're…warm. I feel safe in your arms instead of scared. And someone just tried to kill me."

He smiled. "I don't think love is about feeling comfortable. I think love needs a little fear in order to be all-consuming. We were always meant to be friends, Penny. And I know your memories aren't all there. But we made a good decision to stay friends. The right decision. I love my wife. And you love your husband."

I blinked away the tears in my eyes. Did I love James? The dreams and memories made it seem like I did. My head was trying to catch up to my heart. It almost felt like my heart was beating faster to try and force my mind to speed up too. "I missed my chance with you, huh?" I laughed, but it sounded forced.

"And it was for the best. I hate to think about what would have happened if you chose me. Scarlett and Axel wouldn't exist. Liam wouldn't exist."

Liam. I instinctively moved my hand to my stomach. God, I remembered the feeling of him kicking me. He did it nonstop. He was such a little terror. I had held him in the hospital this morning but I hadn't really known him. But I knew him now. I remembered reading to my stomach and singing to him. The old memories collided with the new ones and I felt like I was going to be sick. "Is he going to be okay? Is my baby going to be okay?"

Tyler pressed his lips together. He didn't have an answer for me. No one did.

I couldn't hold back my tears now. I needed to get to Liam. I needed to hold him again. I needed him to know how much I loved him.

Tyler leaned down and hugged me again. Like a good friend, he knew when I needed a hug. I got another wave of grass and sunshine and my head spun. It was like my memories were vomiting out, one after the next.

I remembered eating lunch with him at Grottos. I remembered him dressing up like Westley from The Princess Bride. I remembered dancing with him. Laughing with him. Hurting him. I swallowed hard. My mind felt like it flipped over as one memory swam to the surface and stuck.

I put my hand on the center of my chest. No one had ever told me that when your heart breaks it actually hurts. It felt like my chest was caving in. I took a deep, shaky breath.

"God, Penny, I'm so sorry." I looked up at Tyler rushing toward me. My eyes immediately landed on the bruise along the left side of his jawbone. The scruff on his chin didn't hide it nearly as well as he probably hoped. I quickly wiped away the rest of my tears.

"What the hell happened to your face?"

"It's nothing." He immediately put his arms around me. "Are you okay?"

"No, I'm not okay. Let me see your face." But he kept his arms wrapped firmly around me.

He ran his hand up and down my back. "I'm fine. God, you're soaked. Let me..."

"You're not fine." I pushed on the middle of his chest until he let me back up a fraction of an inch. He didn't need to say anything. I knew. It was written all over his face. I lightly touched the side of his jaw with my fingertips. "James did that, didn't he?"

"There may have been an altercation late last night."

I closed my eyes. "Tyler, I'm so, so sorry." Mason was with James. Apparently none of his friends were good at keeping him out of trouble. It also meant Ian had probably driven him there when I specifically told him not to take James anywhere. But Ian didn't have to listen to me. I was never his boss.

"There's nothing to apologize about." Tyler put his hand on the back of my head and pressed my face to his chest. There was something so comforting about being in Tyler's arms. Despite his move to New York and all his success, he still smelled the same. Like freshly cut grass and mint. I wasn't even sure how that was possible. There was barely any grass in New York and he wasn't a landscaper. I wrapped my arms around his back. It was selfish, but I needed this right now. I needed my friend. I could tell Tyler wanted to talk, but I wrapped my arms tighter around him. I just needed a few more seconds.

Tyler kissed the top of my head and ran his fingers through my hair. "It's going to be okay, Penny."

No. It's not. *I shook my head against his chest and let my arms drop from his back.*

He grabbed my shoulders and pushed me back so he could look at my face. There was so much hope in his blue eyes. And it killed me.

"How much do you know about what happened?" I asked.

"Everything I need to know."

"Which is?"

"That you and James broke up. And that he thinks I convinced you to run away with me." He searched my face.

So Rob really hadn't talked to James. Neither had his parents. He didn't know. Or maybe he didn't believe them either.

"So now I'm here to actually convince you to run away with me." He lightly touched the bottom of my chin so that I'd look into his eyes.

A part of me wanted to say yes. I wanted to feel the comfort of his arms around me. And see that smile that always made me smile too. The only problem was that I didn't love Tyler. It wouldn't be fair to him or...fuck, Melissa. "I'm still in love with him," I said.

Tyler shook his head. "You broke up. You left him and New York. You're standing in the rain crying because of him. And I'm here for you. We can go wherever you want. We can start a new life together."

"I'm still in love with him," I said again, a little quieter.

He let go of my shoulders. "Okay, but that feeling will fade. You have to move forward."

I shook my head.

"What, so you're going to go through your whole life missing him?"

"What else am I supposed to do, Tyler? He was it for me. There is nothing after him. I was ready to give my whole life to him. That feeling doesn't just disappear after a fight."

"Be with me. I'm right here. I've always been here for you. I'd never do anything to hurt you. Let me fill that void."

"I can't."

"Why? I know you love me. We're great together. I know you felt it back in school. I know you can feel it again."

"I could never hurt Melissa like that."

"We already broke up."

"What?"

"I broke up with her before I came here."

"Why did you do that? You only just started dating." God, she's going to hate me.

"I thought you were getting married. I was at peace with that. Or in denial or something. These past few years haven't been a lie, I was your friend. I enjoyed being your friend." He scratched the back of his neck with his hand. *"But when I found out you two broke up, all I wanted to do was see you. I think I had buried my feelings. I don't know. But I just knew I needed to see you. I never stopped loving you, Penny. And I'll never stop loving you."*

I shook my head back and forth.

"I didn't want this to happen. All I've ever wanted was for you to be happy. I thought that James was that for you, so I just accepted where I was. But when I found out it was over...it feels like my second chance. Our second chance."

"I'm sorry. But it's like you just said. Except, I never stopped loving him. And I'll never stop loving him."

"I can wait. I'm used to waiting. I'll wait my whole life for you, Penny. Don't you see that?" He put his hand on the side of my face.

"Tyler, I don't want you to wait."

"Don't say that. I know you need time to heal from this. I'll wait until you're ready."

"I'll never be ready."

He shook his head. "I love you. Tell me to stay. Choose me. Penny, please give us a chance. I need you. Meet me halfway."

"You don't need me. You need some sweet girl who will put you first. Who thinks the sun rises and sets with you. You deserve that. I can't give you that."

"I'll take whatever you can give me."

"All I can offer you is friendship. Honestly, Tyler, you're my best friend. You've always been there for me..."

"I can't be your friend anymore." He let his hand fall from my cheek. "I thought I could be. But now? No. I need more than that. I can't live my whole life in denial."

"I'm sorry."

He shoved his hands into his pockets. "So...Chicago?"

I nodded. "My new flight leaves tonight. I think maybe I need to do a little soul searching."

"And you know for sure that what you're looking for isn't me?" He gave me a sheepish smile that ripped my heart in half. "How are you so sure?"

I pressed my lips together. There was something else that I hadn't told him. But I didn't want to. It wasn't fair. It was just in my head.

"Tell me." I shook my head. He grabbed my hand. "Tell me. If it's something I can fix..."

"No." I swallowed hard. "Seeing you reminds me that it's my fault that James broke up with me. Because I insisted on being your friend. I made this happen."

"It hurts you to see me?" I closed my eyes and nodded. He dropped my hand. "I'd do anything for you. You know that right?"

I wiped away the tears that had started to fall down my cheeks again.

"Penny, look at me."

I slowly opened my eyes. The hurt on his face was palpable.

"Everything in my gut is telling me to stay and fight for you. But if you want me to leave, I'll leave. Is that what you want?"

"I'm sorry."

His Adam's apple rose and fell. "I can't be your friend anymore."

"I know."

He nodded his head. "I guess this is goodbye then?"

"Where are you going to go?" I thought about his apartment in New York. Melissa was probably waiting there, seething. Hating both of us.

"I think maybe I need a fresh start too," he said. "Some-where...sunnier."

I nodded. "I hope you find what you're looking for."

"I already found what I was looking for," Tyler said with a sigh. "Now...now I'm running away because it hurts too fucking much."

"Tyler..."

"Go back to New York, Penny. Don't spend your whole life missing him. It's exhausting to deny yourself what you want, to spend your whole life dreaming about what you're missing."

The fact that he was talking about me made my chest hurt even more.

"I really hope that you two work it out," he said.

"Thanks, Tyler." I took a step toward him to hug him goodbye, but he immediately took a step back.

"Bye, Penny." He turned around and walked away from me. I watched him climb back into his car. I lifted my hand to wave goodbye, but he didn't look back as he pulled away from the curb and out of my life.

I took a deep breath like I had just woken up in the middle of a nightmare. Tyler was looking down at me with concern etched across his face.

"I hurt you," I said. "All those years ago I hurt you and I'm so sorry. I'm so so sorry."

He smiled. "It's in the past, Penny. I know it probably feels more recent to you, but it was a long time ago."

"So you swear that you're happy?"

"I swear that I'm happy. All that hurt led me to happiness with the right person. Everything has a funny way of working out for the best. Does this mean that you remember breaking my heart and choosing James?" He smiled down at me.

I didn't know whether to nod or to shake my head. Pieces were all that I had. Fragments of a life I had forgotten. But there was no denying the memory that I just had of Tyler. How I felt after James called off our wedding. That devastation. "I remember loving him so much that it felt like I died when he asked me to leave and never come back. Like I didn't know how to keep breathing in a world where he wasn't beside me."

"Imagine how the poor guy has been feeling for the last few days."

I nodded. God, he was right. I had been so focused on my thoughts, when my heart had been leading me to him the whole time. "I don't want to fight the memories anymore. I want to go home."

"Welcome back, Penny." He leaned down and placed a kiss on my forehead like he had all those years ago. A friendship kiss. Nothing more and nothing less.

Tyler may have saved me tonight, but he wasn't my knight in shining armor. James was. He always had been. He saved me when I didn't even realize I needed saving. And if that wasn't a sign that he was my soul mate, what on earth was? I didn't need all my memories to see that.

"As soon as we talk to the police we can get you home. They'll have some questions. And Dr. Nelson will finally be in custody."

He hadn't stirred at all. Tyler must have really knocked him out.

"You're okay, right? You're not hurt at all?"

"I feel fine." Besides for the overwhelming feeling that I missed my family. I desperately wanted to be with them.

"I should call James. He's probably worried sick about you."

I grabbed his arm as he pulled his cell phone out of his pocket. "We can tell him in person. He'll freak out about this more if I'm not right there. He worries so much about me." *He worries? I know that?* I smiled to myself.

"You're probably right. If you want we can stop by my place and get you in a pair of comfy sweatpants. You're drenched from the rain."

I laughed. "You always let me borrow your sweatpants when I come over?" I said it like a question, but I knew it was true. I didn't have a memory of it, but I just knew.

"That's right. It's all coming back."

It was. "If it's okay, I just want to go home." I needed to see James. I needed to tell him that I was remembering. I wanted to hug Scarlett and hold Liam. I wanted my life back. It was like I had finally awakened from a dream. This life around me was real. And I didn't want it any other way. I'd take it just the way it was, even without all my memories.

CHAPTER 5

Monday - *Penny*

Tyler sat with me on the taxi ride back to my apartment. And insisted on walking me all the way to my door. It was like he was afraid I was going to be snatched again. Thanks to him, that wasn't going to happen.

I lifted my hand to knock, but I stopped and turned to him before my knuckles collided with the wood. "Thank you again, Tyler. No matter how many times I say it, it'll never be enough."

"Get inside before you catch a cold. James will kill me if you get the flu on top of everything else."

I smiled. "I think you'll be in James' good graces permanently after tonight."

"Maybe I'll finally get that A."

I laughed. "Psh. You got an A in my book. And you probably would have if I didn't get our class canceled."

"Fair point. Go on," he gestured to the door. "Get back to your life."

It did feel like I was delaying. As soon as I went through that door, everything would change. Or go back to the way it was? My memories still felt like dreams instead of reality. But I wanted this. I wanted this amazing life. I don't know how I wound up here, but I was so ecstatic that I had.

Reading about James' love and experiencing it were going to be two very different things. I wanted to feel what I felt in the pages of my novel. I wanted to know what it was like to be truly loved and love in return. I was ready. I knocked on the door.

It flew open in a matter of seconds.

"Penny!" Melissa screamed and threw her arms around me. I swore she even lifted me up in the air a little. "Jesus! I thought you were dead in a ditch. Or worse." She squeezed me so hard that it hurt. "Where the hell have you been?"

God, what would be worse than being dead? She didn't give me a chance to respond to her question. She let me go and stared at Tyler over my shoulder. And then back at me.

Disappointment crossed her face. "You were with Tyler? We called him a million times. We called you a million times!" she yelled at him.

"Penny wanted to talk to James in person about what happened," he said. "She thought it would be better this way."

"Better what way?" Melissa let go of me. "Did you two...are you two..." She shook her head. "Penny, you're making a mistake. You and James are meant to be together. You just need to give it more time."

What the hell was she talking about? Did she think Tyler and I were here together so that we could confess our undying love for each other to James? Why would she think that?

I glanced up at all the people gathering in the foyer. Everyone. And I recognized their faces. Hailey, Tyler's wife. Beautiful, perfect Hailey that fixed the heart I had broken. And Bee and Mason. Matt. Rob and Daphne. Jen and Ian. My parents and James' father. All the kids were missing but I knew it was late. Really late. I looked around once more, but it actually wasn't everyone. James was missing.

"How could you, Tyler?" Melissa said. "How could you?" Her voice was filled with disgust.

Tyler held up both his hands like he was innocent. Which he was. God, this really was not how I pictured tonight going. I wanted to come home and tell James everything. Tell him how I felt. I wanted a quiet night alone and he wasn't even here. But everyone else in the world was.

"Melissa, just stop for a second, okay? Nothing is going on with me and Tyler. Dr. Nelson attacked me on my way back here after my walk. Luckily Tyler was on a run and saw the whole thing. He followed us and saved me. Dr. Nelson is in jail. It's over. It's all over. Where is James?" I felt like I was breaking. "I need to see him. I'm remembering. I remember him." My lip started to tremble. "Where is he?"

Everyone was eerily quiet.

"He went to go see our mother," Rob said when no one else spoke. "He thought...we thought..." his voice trailed off. "It wouldn't have been the first time that her actions hurt you guys."

"He's with his mother? Right now?" *Poor, James.* He had given up on her after our wedding. They hadn't spoken in years. Going to her would have been really hard for him. "He went alone?" Why would they send him alone?

Rob nodded. "He said it was something he had to handle on his own."

I had been making James feel so alone ever since I woke up. Combining that feeling with seeing his mom? That wasn't going to be good. It would have been easy for me to call him and tell him to come home. But if he was going to see his mom, that was a big step. And I needed to be by his side. He needed me and I was finally ready to be needed. "Can someone take me to them?"

Rob didn't ask why I didn't want to just call. He just agreed without a second thought.

I didn't thank everyone for worrying about me. I didn't thank them for coming together to search for me. All I could think about was James. I turned and walked right back out the door with Rob on my tail.

***

"When did you start to remember?" Rob asked as he took another turn.

Rain was pounding so hard against the windshield that the wipers barely looked like they were working.

"I was having dreams. I didn't…I didn't realize that they were actually memories."

James' parents had sold their house after the divorce. I remembered being sad about it because it meant James' tree house would disappear. We had visited it one more time before the house went on the market. He assured me that he wasn't going to miss it. And that maybe one day we'd have a house with a yard and that he'd build a tree house for Scarlett. I absentmindedly touched my stomach. Liam now too. The thought made me feel sick. Part of me wanted to tell Rob to drive toward the hospital instead, but I had a feeling that right at this moment my husband needed me more than my baby. I felt drawn to the outskirts of the city. The sprawling lawns and ornate houses. James was here. Somewhere.

"How long has your mother been back in town?" I asked.

"I don't know. I didn't even realize that she was. James knew I guess." He kept his eyes on the road.

James knew. I wondered if he missed her. If he ever thought about forgiving her. She had never even met Scarlett. My heart felt like it was breaking. What if she never got a chance to meet Liam? I blinked away my tears as I stared out the window.

"Do you remember me then?" Rob asked.

I knew he was trying to lighten the mood. I turned to look at him and it was like I saw flashes of our past. Which contained a lot of me playfully shoving his shoulder and him cheesing way too hard. "Yeah. You're the brother that makes me laugh until my stomach hurts."

A smile spread across his face. "The better brother."

"That's debatable."

He laughed. "No, it's a fact."

"Riiiiight." I bit the inside of my lip. He really was good at making me laugh. So maybe he could tell me about Liam in a way that wouldn't make me feel like throwing up. "How's Liam doing?"

All I could hear was the rain on the windshield again.

"I don't know, Penny. But he's a fighter." He glanced at me out of the corner of his eye. "Like both his parents."

CHAPTER 6
Monday - *James*

My mom was holding her front door open and staring at me like I was a stranger. Maybe I was to her now. She seemed the same to me, though.

"James," she finally said.

"Mother." The word sounded strange coming out of my mouth. I hadn't used it in so long. Except to refer to Penny as "your mom" to Scarlett. The fact that each of them held that title was shocking. Penny was so loving and kind. And my mother? Well, she was the kind of mother that just stood there instead of hugging you. Like she was doing right now.

"What are you doing here?" She didn't invite me in even though I was literally standing in the rain.

"Penny's missing." My voice cracked. "I don't know if you heard about the incident a few weeks ago..."

"Of course I heard. It was all over the news."

I nodded. "I think the same guy has kidnapped her. I just...I wanted to know..."

"You think I had something to do with it?" She lifted her chin slightly so that she was looking down her nose at me.

I felt like I was a child again that was being scolded. "I just needed to ask. I needed to make sure."

"I told you I was sorry about what happened with Isabella. I told you and you didn't believe me. I'm not the monster you're making me out to be. I've been nothing but a good mother to you."

"A good mother? You forced me to marry someone I didn't care about. You told me no one would ever care about me, only my money."

"I was looking out for you. And I was right, wasn't I?"

"Penny didn't marry me for my money." I didn't know why I was having this conversation with her. We'd never see eye to eye. Whereas the rain made me feel close to Penny, the rain falling between my mother and me felt like an insurmountable distance. "She fell in love with me for me."

"And how did that work out for you? That whole amnesia thing? Probably a ruse for a divorce. And she'll get half of everything. She'll ruin you and drag our name through the mud. She's never been anything but a nuisance."

"I've thought about reaching out to you so many times. And up until tonight I've always made the right choice." I shook my head and turned away from her. I started to walk down the front steps of the enormous house she bought with her settlement money. Her heart was as empty as all the rooms inside.

"I don't know what you want from me, James!" she yelled after me. "You want me to care after you've shut me out for over four years? You haven't even let me meet my grandchildren. You won't let me hold my only grandson before he might pass? I'm not the monster here. You are."

I figured she knew about Liam. Jen was still in contact with her. But to hear her throw my son's health in my face as a bargaining tool? No fucking way. I was done. I turned around and walked back up the stairs. "If you cared, you would have called. You would have come to the hospital to see if he was okay. I don't know how many days Liam has left. But I'm going to make sure that he's only surrounded by people who love him for every single one of those days."

"And that's me," she said.

I was shocked to see tears in her eyes.

"Why do you think I moved back here? I wanted to be close to you again. To Rob. To my grandchildren."

Why now? "Penny is part of that. You didn't bother to show up to Rob's wedding. And you haven't even met Daphne. You..."

"I wasn't invited." She sniffed. "He didn't invite me, James. My own son didn't invite me to his wedding."

I didn't know that. I knew that Rob had my back after what happened. But I didn't know he didn't send her a wedding invitation.

"I confess, I didn't think Penny was a good choice for you. I thought Isabella was a better fit. Status wise." She pressed her lips together. "But I was trying. I was making an effort. But then she poisoned your mind after your wedding. She took you away from me. And Rob too. And all my grandchildren. She took everything away from me. She drove a wedge between us."

"You did that all by yourself."

She nodded like she actually agreed with what I said.

"Penny and I are a package deal. If you don't want her in your life then you can't have me or your grandchildren either."

"Okay. I'll apologize to her."

"You can't just save face. You have to mean it. I think you'll find that she's really easy to love. Trust me. I fell for her harder and faster than I ever thought possible."

"I'll mean it. I'm turning a new leaf, James. You'll see." She wiped away the tears in her eyes. "Can I come back with you tonight to see Liam?" she asked. "And Scarlett?"

I shook my head. "I have to find Penny."

"Well, where have you looked?"

"I've called everyone I could think of. Even friends from her past. I've been to all her favorite places in the city. She ran out on me a few days ago and went to Newark. But I don't think that's what this was. It seemed like she was starting to remember. I could see it in her eyes. I think something must have happened to her on her walk. And I'm tired. I'm so tired." I felt myself breaking. My mom was smiling at me and acting human. "I need her, Mom. I need her and I can't even explain how much."

It was like I couldn't stop talking. I just kept going and going. Maybe it was because my mom was smiling at me for once. Or maybe it was because it finally felt like she cared. "These past few weeks have felt like a nightmare that I can't wake up from. I just need to find her. And then worry about fixing everything after I tell her how much I love her. If something's happened to her, I don't know if I can keep going. She's everything to me."

"Try looking behind you," my mom said. The smile on her face was probably brighter than I had ever seen it.

I turned around. Penny was standing at the bottom of the steps looking up at me. The rain hitting the pavement was causing steam to float around her. She looked like an angel. Maybe that's what she was. After all, she had saved me.

"Penny." It felt like time slowed as I ran down the stairs.

She tucked a loose strand of hair behind her ear. "I'm sorry, I didn't want to disrupt your moment, I..."

I pulled her into my arms and kissed her harder than I meant to. The way I used to. The way I knew she loved. I knew it was too much. I knew she was seconds away from pushing me back. From telling me she didn't remember. That I was going too fast.

That she needed time. But I needed this. For just one second I needed this.

But she surprised me by kissing me back. And not just a timid, unfamiliar kiss. It was her. A kiss that I was used to. A kiss that reminded me of my version of Penny.

She pulled away far too soon. "I love you, James." She took my face between her hands and stared into my eyes. "I love you with all my heart. I only remember pieces of our life, but I know that much is true. You're my everything too. Every. Single. Thing."

Her fingertips pressed harder against my jaw with each word she spoke, like she was trying to cling on to the present.

"You came back to me." My lips met hers again.

"I'm sorry it took me so long. I'm sorry I fought my heart. I'm so so sorry, James." She wrapped her arms around the back of my neck to pull me closer to her.

"You've always loved apologizing when you've done nothing wrong."

She laughed. "You don't have to use the same lines on me anymore. I'm remembering. I remember you saying that."

"And do you remember why you like the rain now?" I held her tight against my chest as it poured.

"We met on a rainy morning. And you walked me home in the rain one night. You were there when I needed you. You have been ever since. And our first kiss was in the rain. I'm pretty sure I fell in love with you in a storm. Isn't that how our love has always been? Chaotic and scary and all-consuming? That kind of love? A love worth fighting for?"

I smiled down at her. "A love worth fighting for."

She leaned closer and whispered in my ear. "I remember your mom not exactly being fond of me. Any chance that's changed?"

"I think maybe it just did."

She kissed the scruff on my jaw line. "Well, good. I'm a big proponent of second chances. And third ones." She looked up with hopeful eyes. "I should probably go say hi, right?"

I saw more than hope in her eyes as she stared at me. I saw love. I saw her. I took a deep breath. God I had missed her looking at me like that. Instead of letting her go, I hugged her harder. I wasn't sure I'd ever let her out of my arms again.

CHAPTER 7

Monday - *Penny*

I felt like I was dreaming. The rain hitting the asphalt caused clouds of steam to surround us, encasing us in a haze. His face was blurry in front of me, but I knew it was because of my tears instead of the rain.

I had tried to push him away. I had tried to push love away. I couldn't apologize enough. I wanted to get down on my hands and knees and beg him for forgiveness. But he was holding me so tightly that I couldn't move an inch. I could barely even breathe. And I wouldn't change a thing.

How many times had he held me like this in the past? I was seeing flashes of moments. Pieces of a puzzle that didn't quite fit together. But it was enough. Just being in his arms would always be enough for me.

"I can't live without you, Penny." His voice was muffled in my hair. "I can't breathe without you."

His words caused more jumbled memories to collide, one after the next, until a longer one stuck. I could see it like it was yesterday, with the same cool rain falling around us.

"I do trust you." He looked up into the sky.

A raindrop hit my forehead. I looked up too. The drops fell faster until it was full on raining.

He abruptly stood up. "Let's get back to the car," he said.

Not when I was this close. "James, tell me."

"You're going to get a cold."

"James, tell me!"

"I've already told you. More or less." He put his hand through his hair. He looked completely distraught. "I thought you understood."

"Understood what?" I felt so dense. "What am I not the answer to?" I stood up. "What did she mean when she said to stop running? What are you running from? Don't push me away again. Don't do what she said you would."

"I was trying to protect you. I told you that."

"But what are you trying to protect me from? Why do you think I shouldn't be with you? It can't possibly be that bad. Just tell me what it is."

"Damn it, Penny." He pulled me against his chest and kissed me. It was angry and hard and hot. His hands slid to the small of my back. He pushed my shirt up slightly so that his palm was against my skin.

"Stop." I pushed on his chest. He was so manipulative. "Stop using sex as a weapon."

"I don't..." He looked at my face and released me from his grip. He took a step back from me. "I didn't realize I was doing that."

What I had said seemed to hurt his feelings. But I couldn't dwell on it right now. That wasn't what I wanted to talk about. "Tell me what you're hiding. You told me no more secrets. Don't you want us to work? Tell me!"

"I have told you! I told you that I was drunk all of college. I told you that I've had sex with dozens of women. I told you I threw myself into my career in order to avoid my life. Everything I did was so that I didn't have to face reality. Whatever horrible thing you can think of, I've probably done it. I told you I wasn't a good man. I told you that."

I swallowed hard. The rain against my face felt soothing. I wasn't sure what to say. I did know all that. That couldn't be what he was hiding.

"I'm an addict, Penny." He looked so young and so vulnerable.

What? *He didn't drink that much. He didn't seem like an addict to me at all. He usually seemed calm and collected and completely in control. And then Isabella's words came back to me. I didn't see it because he wasn't addicted to drugs or booze right now. He was addicted to me.* **I'm his drug?**

"Penny? Say something."

"All this talk about forever..."

"I mean it."

"But what happens when you get bored with me? Will you go off chasing your next high?"

"No." He lowered his eyebrows. *"I'm not addicted to you. It's different with you, it's not the same."*

"How do you know?"

"I was trying to avoid my life. I was miserable. Every day I felt like I was suffocating. I needed an escape. But I'm happy now."

"Because of me? Or because of teaching? Or what?"

"It was my decision to come here."

"Because you walked in on Isabella..."

"Yes. But I came here for me. I'm living the way I want to live. I'm not answering to anyone else. I don't need an escape anymore."

"Isabella said you needed to get help."

"I've gotten help."

"So you're not addicted to drugs, or alcohol, or work, or...sex anymore?"

"No. I haven't been addicted to anything since I left the city. I was living a life that wasn't mine there. I was numb. Those things made me feel alive. They sustained me. They were a choice I could make for myself."

"So you chose to do them? That doesn't make you an addict, James. If you had control over your choices..."

"I couldn't stop, Penny. Whenever I was able to pull myself out of one thing, I just moved on to the next." His words hung in the air. *"Don't look at me like that. I'm not addicted to you. I'm not going to move on. I need you in my life. I need you, Penny."*

THIS IS LOVE

He needs me. *All of his words now seemed to have a double meaning. But didn't I need him too? When he didn't talk to me for weeks I was a complete mess. My world had become isolated and cold. And I had hated it. I hated my life without him.*

"Penny, I've made so many mistakes. But I was young and stupid."

"You're still young."

"Okay. But I'm not stupid anymore." *He gave me a forced smile.*

"Addicts are like...it's not something that goes away, is it?"

"No, it's not."

"So, how do you control it?" *I felt stupid asking these questions. The age gap between us suddenly felt larger than before. He was an adult, with adult problems. All I was worried about was my next Stat test. And now him.*

He lowered his eyebrows slightly. "My therapist helps me with that."

"You have a therapist?"

"I do." *His eyes searched my face.* "He doesn't think I'm addicted to you either."

"You talk about me?"

"Yes."

"He knows that you're dating a student?"

"Doctor patient confidentiality. He did advise me against it. I think he's glad that I ignored his advice though."

"Why?"

"I'm happier when we're together. Everyone can see that."

It was weird, standing in the rain so far apart. It made me feel so separate from him. I didn't like that feeling. "Why didn't you just tell me?"

"Because I liked the way you looked at me. Like I was strong and in control. It made me feel like I could be those things for you. I thought everyone could see my demons when they looked in my eyes. You never did. You just saw me. I didn't want that to change."

"I don't think any differently of you." *His words made me want to cry. I didn't have much self confidence. I thought he was the opposite of me. But we*

- 63 -

were more alike than I thought. He was so broken. I didn't want him to feel that way.

"You do. You're looking at me right now like I'm weak."

"I don't think that you're weak. You're incredibly strong for overcoming something like that."

He put his hands in his pockets. We were both completely drenched. He was staring at me. The distance between us was unbearable.

"I don't want you to leave me," he said slowly. "But if this is too much..."

"No. James." I closed the distance between us. "I'll never let you go."

"I'm not addicted to you."

"You keep saying that. And all I can think about is how rude it sounds." I smiled at him.

"I don't understand how you can keep choosing me. I'm..."

"Perfect. Everything that you've been through has made you who you are. And I love the man I see in front of me. I love you so much."

It started raining harder. "I'm divorced." He almost had to yell it over the rain.

"I know."

"No more of this waiting nonsense?"

"No. My heart is yours."

He was smiling down at me. "I'm divorced!" He picked me up and twirled me around.

I laughed as he set me back down on my feet. I rubbed my palm against the scruff on his cheek. "You're all mine."

"All yours, Miss Taylor." He turned his head and kissed my palm.

Miss Taylor. That wasn't my name anymore. That wasn't me. I was Mrs. James Hunter. And I couldn't live without the man in front of me. I couldn't breathe without him either.

"My heart is yours," I mumbled into his chest. "Forever and always. It's yours, James."

He held me even tighter, if that was possible.

I wasn't the same vulnerable girl from my memories. I was strong. I was whole. I was a wife. And a mother. All the memories came to a halt. "Liam." My voice came out like a croak as I pulled away from James' embrace. "We have to go to Liam." I remembered him. I remembered him kicking me constantly. And I remembered knowing he'd be a little boy. I knew it. And now he was here and he hadn't really met me. The real me.

"You're soaked," James' mother said. "Come inside. I'll have Helga dry your clothes. And then we can all go see him together, okay?"

It felt like I was running out of time. Like I needed to see him right this second. As if there was a clock ticking down in my head approaching zero. "No, I need to see my son. He doesn't know...he doesn't know how much..."

James grabbed both sides of my face. "How much you love him? He knows, baby. Take a deep breath for me. My mother is right. We've both just been through surgery. We can't afford to get sick on top of everything else. Liam needs us to be strong right now."

Surgery. Surgery. The words echoed around in my head. "James." I placed my hand on the left side of his chest. *God, James.* I could feel his heart beating through his shirt. "James." My voice cracked.

"Let's get in out of the rain."

My dreamlike state returned as he guided me into the house. His mom started talking and pointing but I didn't hear anything she said. But I did register the fact that she smiled at me. I had never seen her smile at me before. Right?

James and I walked into a guest bedroom. I had a million things I needed to tell him. He didn't know about Dr. Nelson. He didn't know what pieces of us I remembered. I had apologized, but he didn't really know how sorry I was. How could I put it into words? How could I ever apologize enough?

"Penny?"

He pulled me out of my thoughts. The way he was staring at me made it seem like I had missed something. Like he had been trying to get my attention for some time. He was staring at me expectantly. I didn't want to miss any more moments. I had already missed so much. I wanted to apologize again. I wanted him to hold me again. Kiss me again. But there was a distance between us. I thought we had just closed it. But in this cold, unfamiliar room? I felt it. Like there was a crack in the ground separating us.

"Hop in the shower to warm up. We can talk afterward. If you want," he quickly added. "It's fine if you don't want to." He gave me a small smile that for some reason looked sad.

What had I missed? What had he been trying to ask me?

"Leave your clothes out here so I can give them to my mom's maid," he said before I could ask. "I'll go grab you a towel. And just...let me know when you're done, okay? There's another shower down the hall that I'm going to use real quick."

I remembered showering with him. I remembered doing that a lot. But we weren't alone. We were at his estranged mother's house. And she and Rob were both waiting for us. This wasn't the time or place for us to reconnect. But I so badly wanted to reach for him. My body didn't move though. And my throat didn't seem to be able to work. So I just nodded. My apology from earlier definitely wasn't enough. How could it have been? I almost ruined us. And I felt the distance between us reverberating through my soul.

I turned away from him. We weren't okay. Would we ever be okay again? Tears welled in my eyes as I closed the bathroom door behind me. I waited for the water to run scalding hot before I stepped under its stream. It should have burned my skin, but I barely felt it.

It was like the steam was choking me. Like it was everything I had done in the past week trying to push me down. "I'm sorry, I'm sorry." I couldn't breathe. What had I done? What a fucking mess I had made. "I'm sorry." My knees buckled and I fell to the tiled floor of the shower. "I'm sorry." My son was alone in a hospital fighting for his life when I didn't remember him. "I'm sorry." My daughter tried to accept the imposter that I was, but missed her actual mother. "I'm sorry." And James? *James.* I tried to leave him. I tried to dismiss the life we had built together. I broke us. "I'm sorry."

I heard the bathroom door squeak open and swallowed a huge gulp of air even though it didn't seem to fill my lungs.

"I have the towels." James' voice was quiet through the steam and the sound of the water.

"I'm sorry," I mumbled to the floor. I wanted him to be able to hear me, but I was out of strength. My whisper disappeared into the steam.

"Penny?"

"I'm sorry," I said again.

The shower door opened but I kept staring at the tiled floor.

"Jesus." His hands were on me in a matter of seconds, trying to help me back to my feet, but I resisted his help.

"I'm sorry. I'm sorry."

"Baby, it's okay," he said in the voice he used for Scarlett. Like I was just some innocent child that had done nothing wrong. But that wasn't true. I had done everything wrong.

"None of this okay!" I couldn't breathe. "I broke us. I broke us."

"You didn't break us. I'm right here." His hands gripped my shoulders. "You came back to me. That's all that matters."

"But I tried so hard to push you away."

"And failed. You failed. I've never wanted you to fail in anything you do except this. You failed at this one thing, and I'm so grateful. Penny, look at me."

I couldn't look up at him. "How could you possibly keep loving me despite how awful I was?"

"Because that wasn't you. You weren't you. It's okay."

"It's not okay! I was awful! I tried to leave. I…" I was choking on my words. "I wanted to leave everything behind. I wanted to leave you. I wanted to start a new life that had nothing to do with this one. How can you just stand there saying it's okay?"

He knelt down on the floor with me. "Oh, baby." He cradled my face in his hands and tilted my face up so that I'd look at him. "That never would have happened. There's no way you could live without me."

It was such a cocky thing to say. But he didn't say it in an arrogant way. He said it as he stared deep into my eyes. He said it because it was true.

My eyes dropped to the towel that was wrapped around his waist. And the perfect V line that dipped beneath the towel. I remembered this. I remembered us. But a memory was so different from reality. I wanted to experience him. And there was no better apology than a blowjob. I had heard that phrase before. From Rob maybe? Who the fuck cared. I wanted James to know that I loved him. That I'd always love him. That I was so fucking sorry.

I grabbed the knot in his towel and pulled.

He reached down to hold it in place.

"You're healing, Penny. We can't..."

"I need you. I feel like I can't breathe. This...this will show me that we're okay. This..." I pulled harder, but he gripped the towel tighter too. It didn't budge.

I swallowed hard. I remembered the sex being amazing. I knew that he was perfection underneath that towel. But he wasn't offering that to me. He didn't want me. And I honestly couldn't remember a time when he didn't want me. It felt like my heart couldn't beat any faster. That my cheeks couldn't be any redder. I swallowed hard. *He doesn't want you anymore, Penny. You ruined every-thing.*

I pulled my hand back like his skin had stung me. Of course he didn't love me anymore. He was a Greek god. And I was just...me. The scales were so tipped in his favor that it didn't make any logical sense for us to be together in the first place. Except one thing that wasn't tangible. He loved me. Love bal-anced the scales. But I lost it. I lost him.

Minutes ago he had run down the steps of this house and kissed me like I was his whole world. Now? He had time to real-ize that I wasn't worth it. He had time to see me crying on a bathroom floor. He had seen me. The real me. A literal puddle of the person I once was. And now he knew better than to love me.

I expected him to walk away from me. Instead, he pulled me into his arms and hugged me impossibly tight. And as soon as his arms were around me, I started crying again. I hugged him back. Maybe he didn't want to make love to me anymore, but I'd take what I could get.

"I don't know what else I can say." My words were jumbled by the water falling on top of us. "I don't know how to apologize enough. I wasn't me. And I was horrible to you. But that wasn't me. That's not how I feel. I love you. I love you, James." I was clinging to him so tightly I wasn't sure he could breathe.

"Just don't leave me again." His words almost got lost in the steam, but I heard them. "My heart can't take it. Please stop running away from what we have."

Suddenly everything clicked. Like a million little pieces falling into place. He thought I ran out on him again tonight? That's what he thought? *God.* "James, I didn't run out on you tonight. I didn't. I know I tried to once, but I'd never do that now."

"It's okay, I'm just glad you're back..."

"James, I swear I didn't. I was already starting to remember what we had. It was Dr. Nelson. He attacked me in Central Park."

"What?" The vulnerability in his voice was gone. He pulled back and he looked like he was about to commit murder and end up in a jail cell right beside the one Dr. Nelson was probably sitting in right now.

"It's okay, he's in custody. Dr. Nelson tried to hurt me, but Tyler saw the whole thing. He stopped him."

"Tyler saved you." He said the words slowly like he didn't understand.

"Yeah...I guess you could put it that way." I wasn't sure what he wanted me to say. Yes, Tyler had rescued me. I couldn't exactly sugarcoat the truth.

He just stared at me.

"Technically he did save me. But it was random luck. He just happened to be on a run. I was lucky."

"Tyler." He released me from his embrace. "Of course. I looked everywhere for you, but your fucking knight in shining armor saved the day." He stood up.

"James." I scrambled to my feet and almost slipped on the slick tile. "You're not seriously upset?"

"How am I supposed to feel after I saw that you were reading all about him before you disappeared?"

What was he talking about? "I shuffled the pages around because I read a…" I awkwardly cleared my throat. "I happened to read a heated scene between you and me and didn't want anyone to know where I left off. I guess something else ended up on top?"

"So it was a coincidence that all your encounters with Tyler were spread out all over the coffee table?"

"Yes." Damn, how did that happen? Luck was only on my side once tonight, I guess. I was glad I wasn't dead, but I really freaking wished James wasn't looking at me the way he was right now. The steam in the shower might as well have been coming out of his ears.

"Penny, the reason you didn't tell me your favorite movie was because it reminds you of him. He's your Westley."

I shook my head. "What? No."

"You felt him up while you watched the movie together."

"I don't even know what you're talking about. When? When I was 19? Jesus, James, it's like you said. It's just a dumb movie."

"A dumb movie that the 19-year-old version of you loved."

"Well she fucking sucked. I think we both can agree to that. She was an idiot. The only good thing she ever did was sleep with her professor."

"That's debatable."

I wasn't sad anymore. I was seething. "Which part? That you were the only good decision I made back then? Or that you were even a good decision at all?" I poked him hard in the middle of his chest. "I never asked for you to save me. If I remember correctly, which I feel like I do now, you were never a white knight. You were a dark one. We didn't ride off into the sunset. We fought for our love. Just like I'm doing now. So don't stand there and tell me that we were a mistake all those years ago, because you couldn't be more wrong. You should be thanking Tyler for saving me. I could have been dead. And there's no way you could live without me either, James." I threw his words back at him.

"Do you remember what it's like when I'm mad at you?"

A memory came rushing back.

"Tomorrow I'm going to make love to you." He slid his fingers up the insides of my thighs. "Tell me what you want me to do to you tonight."

"Porter is right inside the door, James. What if he comes up here?"

"The idea of getting caught has always made you want me even more. Besides, he's blocking the door so we won't have any unexpected visitors." He kissed the side of my neck. "I want you to remember tonight. I want you to remember what it was like to choose me because you wanted me, not because we had a slip of paper that said you had to. But because you can't resist me. Because I'm the only one that can make you scream. Because the thought of my cock makes your pussy ache. Because you can't fucking live without me."

I moaned as his fingers brushed against my thong. I could smell the scotch on his breath. I knew he wasn't drunk, though. He was just horny. And God, I was too.

"Tell me, baby. Tell me what you want."

I wanted to go back to where we started. I never wanted that passion to fade. "Fuck me, James. Just like you did in your office that first time."

"I was punishing you that day." His fingers pushed my thong to the side and he gently touched my wetness. "Have you been a bad girl?"

I moaned again as I spread my legs for him.

"Tell me how bad you've been." The tip of his finger slowly encircled me.

His dirty words just made me want him even more. "So bad. Punish me, James."

He grabbed my waist and pulled me off the ledge. He pushed my shirt up. In a matter of seconds I was completely naked. I had only managed to undo all the buttons on his shirt. His hands were still so much more experienced than mine.

"Turn around, Penny."

I stared at his chiseled abs that were barely visible behind his tie. I wanted to reach up and undo it. I wanted to run my fingers along the contours of his muscles.

"Penny. Turn around and put your hands on the ledge. Now."

I loved when he talked to me like that. I loved everything about him. I turned around and placed my hands on the cold concrete ledge. Normally the view would have my full attention. But I could feel him staring at me. It was like every inch of my body was aware of his presence. I arched my back slightly and he groaned from behind me.

He pushed my thighs apart.

"You're so beautiful, baby." His voice sounded tight. He slapped my ass hard.

I lifted my ass higher in the air. I loved the sting of his palm. I loved when he took control of my body. And he loved it too.

"And so fucking naughty." He spanked me again.

I gripped the ledge.

His fingers gently traced where he had just spanked. "You made me wait two and a half fucking years to marry you." He spanked me again. "I hate waiting." He spanked me even harder. His palm stayed pressed against my ass as his other hand slipped between my thighs.

Fuck.

"You're dripping wet, baby." Two of his fingers sunk deep inside of me.

God yes.

"I can feel how much you want me. Beg me for my cock, baby. Tell me how much you need me." He spanked me again.

"James." I was panting now. *"Please."*

He continued to slowly move his fingers in and out of me. His palm landed on my ass harder than it ever had before.

"James!"

"Tell me that you need me!"

Something was wrong. I could hear it in his voice. I could feel it in the way he was holding me. Our conversation from this morning hadn't calmed him down like it had me. He still didn't believe me. If my surrendering to him helped him understand, then fine. I'd always be willing to surrender myself to him. *"I need you."*

"Then why did you walk out on me when I needed you the most?!" He thrust inside of me hard.

Fuck! This morning he had been distraught and lost. And now he was angry.

His fingers dug into my hips as he slammed into me again. *"Why did you not trust me enough to tell me what was happening? Why do you leave me in the dark when I try so hard every day to be your light?"* He grabbed a fistful of my hair to make me arch my back more.

"I'm sorry."

"Why do you refuse to let me protect you?"

I don't know. Tears started to come to my eyes.

"Why? Tell me why!"

"I don't know!" I clenched my jaw. He was being rough, but it didn't hurt. What hurt was that he was right. I hadn't realized I was doing it. But I purposely kept things to myself because I didn't want to add to the constant burden he carried. The one he wouldn't let me help him hold. I didn't want to

add anything else because I was worried he might slip. And I couldn't lose him. I couldn't be the reason that he slipped.

His fingers eased on my hips and one of his hands slid down my stomach. He gently massaged his thumb against my clit.

"I don't like when you lie to me."

"I'm not lying to you. Keep fucking me, James." I needed him to get whatever was in his system out. This was the only way I knew how. I thought making love to him this morning would fix this, but I was wrong. "Make me scream your name. Show me how good this feels. Show me how much you need me too."

He groaned as he thrust into me faster.

"Harder!" I closed my eyes. The intensity was too much. The weight of what this all meant was too much.

"Fuck." He slammed into me as his fingers dug into my skin. "Come for me, Penny."

It was easy to follow his command. All I could feel was him relentlessly fucking me. The mixture of pleasure and pain had almost made me come when we had only just started. "James!" I moaned and pushed back against him. I opened my eyes as I started to come. And I had the strangest sensation that I was flying. The city stretched out below me. And I knew as soon as I came down from this high, the reality of what had just happened would make it feel like I was falling. I wanted to fly for as long as I could. I pushed back against the ledge. James hadn't cum yet. I didn't have to fall yet.

But James immediately pulled out of me.

No.

He grabbed my arm and turned me around. His other hand was slowly pumping up and down his erection. He pushed down on my shoulders until I was kneeling in front of him. I usually liked when he did this. And I knew he liked it. He had told me he liked seeing his cum drip down my breasts. It made me feel sexy too. But it didn't seem like that tonight. He was doing it because he felt insecure. As if this somehow claimed me. Why couldn't he see that I was already his?

His first shot landed on the center of my chest. There was no bliss on his face. Only agony. Two more hit each of my breasts. After his last stream hit my stomach he turned around and quickly started to get dressed. The silence was unnerving.

I wiped off his semen with my t-shirt and then pulled my robe on. "James." I stood up and put my hand on his arm, but he pulled away.

"I'm sorry," he said. "I don't know what came over me. You asked me to punish you and I was thinking of reasons why I should. I got carried away."

Why wasn't he facing me?

He exhaled loudly. "Did I hurt you?"

"No." This time when I touched his arm, he didn't flinch. I walked around him and looked up into his eyes. "Talk to me."

"Why do you keep me in the dark?" He was looking at me like he knew the answer. Like it had been part of the burden he was carrying this whole time.

The thought made me feel so guilty. I had been adding to it when I was trying to do the exact opposite. "Because I'm scared you'll slip. I'm scared if anything ever goes wrong you'll slip. And I won't be able to get you back."

"Well I did." He reached into his pocket. He pulled something out and tossed it to me.

I caught it in my hand. It looked like a small bag of baby powder. "What is this?"

He ran his hand through his hair.

"Tell me you didn't take this, James. Tell me you didn't do this."

"You left me."

"You kicked me out! Tell me you didn't take this!" I threw the bag back at him.

"I didn't take it."

An exasperated laugh escaped my lips. "Don't just say that because it's what I want to hear. Tell me the truth."

"I didn't take it. But the moment that you left...that's when I knew I was addicted to you. That's the moment I knew that I was still sick. I wanted to dull the pain. I wanted something, anything to dull that pain."

"That means you wanted something because you were hurting. That doesn't mean you're addicted to me."

"Don't you get it, Penny? My life sucks without you. I don't need anything to dull the pain when I'm with you because you dull it. You're my drug."

The way he said "you" made my chest hurt.

"It doesn't matter if it's this," *he grabbed the bag off the ground,* "or alcohol or you. I'm an addict. I've always been an addict. And I'll always be an addict. You hide things from me because you're scared of what will happen if I slip. I've already slipped. Every time I fuck you I'm slipping. Can't you see that? Can't you see that I have no fucking control? I almost hurt you..."

"Stop."

"Penny, I can't..."

"Stop!" *My words seemed to echo in the silent night.* "You didn't hurt me. I love when you're rough with me. You fucked me like that because I asked you to. Nothing has changed from this morning. What you see as addiction, I see as love. And the fact that you didn't take whatever is in that bag means you're not an addict."

"Because it wouldn't compare to you! I'm broken, Penny. I'm weak. I'm not worthy of you."

"James." *I tried to keep my voice as even as I could.* "I'm not scared about you slipping because you're weak. I'm scared because I don't know what that side of you is like. All I've ever known is the you that I see in front of me. As far as I'm concerned that's the only you that exists. I'm so sorry I kept you in the dark. I'm sorry that I hurt you. I didn't mean to."

"I know." *He walked past me and put his elbows on the ledge.*

When I had come out here, I thought this moment was so perfect. I wish I could go back in time and ask him to make love to me. Now I was just tired and upset and James was refusing to look at me. This wasn't how it was supposed to be the night before we got married.

"I thought when you found the right person, things were supposed to be easy," he said more to the skyline than to me. "Why does it feel like this relationship is always so much work?"

"I know what you're doing. You're trying to push me away. Again. Like you always do." I leaned against the ledge beside him. "It's like you're stuck in reverse. Why do you not believe in what we have? Why do you keep pushing me away? You and I both know that I didn't walk away from you. This isn't about me. This is about you being scared. And that doesn't make you weak. I'm scared too."

He shook his head.

"Talk to me."

He turned his head to me. "Tomorrow, after I say I do, that's it for me. It's my fresh start. You're my fresh start. If something happens to that, I'm done. I can't live without you. I can't even function without you. You say you don't care if I'm addicted to you. That's your decision. I'm not going to stop you from marrying me because I don't want to. All I've ever wanted was for you to be mine. But yeah, it's fucking terrifying. Because there are no guarantees in life. Who knows what'll happen the next day or the day after that. I've given myself so completely to you that there's nothing left of me without you. There is no me without you."

"James, I feel exactly the same way. And I didn't realize how true that was until our fight last night. And that's why you're feeling that way. Because now you know what it's like to lose me. But I'm not going anywhere."

"You don't know that."

"I'm healthy. And I'm careful. And we have security guards following us around protecting us."

James shook his head. "I'm worried about Isabella. I can't explain it. I just...I know she's planning something. I can feel it. Maybe I'm just unsettled. I realize that no one else thinks Isabella would hurt anyone. But she's out there somewhere, and I'm scared that she'll try."

"We're going to be okay." I put my hand on top of his. "Anything else you need to get off your chest?"

"I want to know that you'll let me protect you."

"I'm letting Porter follow me around. They can hang out with us all the time if that's what you need."

"No, I like being alone with you." He smiled for the first time since we had sex. "I'm sorry." He sighed. "I don't know what's wrong with me. Maybe I'm just finally getting nervous about tomorrow too."

I ducked underneath his arm and let him wrap himself around me. "I promise I'm going to show up."

He laughed. "What about you? Is there anything you need to get off your chest before tomorrow?"

I thought about how I kept things from him before. I wasn't going to do that anymore. "I was wondering if maybe you should call your therapist? I know it's late, so in the morning maybe? To talk to him about the fact that you think you're addicted to me."

"We've already talked about it. He'll say that I'm not."

"So why don't you believe him or me?"

"Because I can't properly express how it felt when you left last night. I can't make someone understand when they don't know how it feels."

"But that's what I've been trying to tell you. I know how it feels. Because I love you."

"Your first reaction wasn't to go out and buy cocaine though."

"Only because I've never done cocaine before. Maybe it would have been. Who knows?"

James laughed. He ran his fingers through my hair. "I'll call him in the morning if it'll make you feel better."

"*I just want you to go into tomorrow knowing that what we have is love,*" I said.

"*Okay. I'll call him. Anything else?*"

I hated bringing up more stuff. But I had to. This had become a night of confessions. There was no point holding back now. "*At the precinct today, that cop said something about how I'd probably have to fill out a lot of restraining orders if I was marrying you. Or something like that. What have you been arrested for, James?*"

"*Nothing that serious.*"

"*Just tell me the list.*"

"*Isabella filed a restraining order against me after I beat up the guy she was screwing behind my back. She said she was scared I'd come after her next. It was ridiculous. I never laid a hand on her. She was just trying to pretend to be the victim.*"

"*Okay.*" That had to be what the officer was referring too. But I wanted to hear it all. "*What else?*"

"*Just minor things.*"

"*Then tell me.*"

He released me from his embrace so he could look down at me. "*It was a long time ago.*"

"*I promise I'm not going to judge you.*"

"*Okay.*" He ran his hand through his hair. "*There were a few fights once or twice that got pretty ugly during summer breaks of college. I hated coming home. I was angry all the time.*" He shook his head. "*I think I got something for peeing in a bush in Central Park once. I don't even really remember. Public drunkenness. I wrote some threatening letters to one of Jen's ex-boyfriends. He deserved it. I don't regret that at all. That was another restraining order. And I've been arrested for being in possession of drugs. Nothing since the restraining order from Isabella, though. Nothing since I've met you.*"

"*How are you not in jail right now?*"

"I have a really good lawyer. And a lot of money."
I shook my head. "So no fights recently?"
"I don't have anything to be angry about anymore."
"You punched Tyler in the face."
"Tyler fucking deserved that."
"He didn't take your money."
"But he wanted you the whole fucking time we were together. And I trusted him. I let you hang out with him every Friday night for the past year because I trusted him."
"He was trustworthy. And he still is. He only ever said anything to me when he realized you broke up with me. Which he found out about because you showed up at his place and punched him in the face. I didn't tell him."
James raised his eyebrow at me.
"Please don't punch anyone else. And don't yell at cops. And don't buy cocaine."
He sighed.
"I feel like those are things most people don't need to be reminded of," I said.
"I'm not most people."
"I know." I touched the side of his face. "You're so much better. Thank you for telling me. Geez, that cop made it seem like you had a rap sheet of beating up women."
"I would never hurt you."
"It hurts me when you try to push me away."
He pulled me back against his chest. "Then I'm done pushing you away." He kissed the top of my head. "I'm sorry that I ruined tonight."
"Tonight was perfect. It finally feels like there's nothing left unspoken between us. Do you have any idea how relieved I feel?"
"I feel it too."
"There is one more thing, though," I said.
I felt his body tense.

"Does a small part of you just want to hop on the next flight out of here and get married somewhere obscure?"

He laughed. "Maybe a small part. If it means I could have you all to myself."

"You already have me all to yourself."

There was so much steam in the shower that I could barely see James a few feet in front of me. His question swirled around in my head. *Do you remember what it's like when I'm mad at you?*

"I remember. But I'm not your fiancée anymore. I'm your wife, James. I'm the mother of your children. And despite what you might think, you don't want to punish me right now. I made you a promise all those years ago that I'd always show up. And here I am. I'm showing up."

He stepped forward so that I could see him clearer. "So what you're saying is that I should be taking care of you?" He put his hand on the center of my chest and pushed me backward until my back hit the cold tiled wall.

My whole body shivered.

"Worshipping your body?"

I swallowed hard.

"You tried to break my heart, Penny."

"You said you forgave me." Right this second, I didn't care if he had or not. He was looking at me in *that* way. The way that had always made my knees weak. The way that gave a girl like me the courage to kiss him during his office hours all those years ago. I never was able to resist him when he looked at me like that.

His hand slid between my breasts, down my stomach, and stopped right where my body needed him the most. "You've forgotten that you spread your legs for me in my office after just one kiss? Don't forget what we once were, Penny. You fucking love being punished. I'm just giving you what you want. What is it that you said?" He ran his thumb against my clit.

"James," I moaned.

He raised his left eyebrow. "No, that wasn't it. I believe it was something about me not being a white knight? I'm a dark one?" The tip of his index finger swirled around my wetness.

I reached out and gripped his shoulders.

"You chose me. You chose the darkness. So don't pretend for a second that you don't love when I spank you. That you don't love when I fuck you so hard you can't walk." He slipped a finger inside of me. "That you don't love when you call me Professor Hunter like it's the dirtiest thing you've ever said."

I moaned as he removed his fingers from my skin.

"This is going to hurt, Penny. But the best part? You're going to love it." He lifted my legs around his waist and then thrust inside of me hard.

The sensation of him filling me made me gasp. *Fuck*. God, I wasn't ready for him. It felt like he was ripping me open. But when he pulled back and thrust in again, I felt a wave of pleasure.

I dug my fingers into the muscles of his back until he pulled them away and pushed the backs of my hands against the cold wall.

No one could love me the way that he could. Emotionally. Physically. It was like his cock was made just for me.

He slammed into me again, harder than before.

Jesus. He was right. I loved that it hurt. I loved the line between pleasure and pain. I fucking loved the way he made me feel. I wasn't the light to his darkness at all. I was as dark as him. I clenched my muscles around his cock, making him groan. No, I wasn't the same girl that fell in love with her professor. I was older, wiser, and had done tons of kegel exercises while I was pregnant. Our sex was great back then. But now? It was fucking amazing. I finally felt like I was as good at pleasing him as he was at pleasing me.

His kisses trailing the side of my neck were so soft compared to the way he was slamming into me. Like he wanted me to feel the love despite the fact that we were fucking. And just as I thought it, he sucked on the side of my neck hard, erasing any feeling of soft intimacy. It felt like a lightning bolt went through me.

And I remembered. I remembered everything. The pain mixed with the pleasure. The smell of his cologne combined with the steam and filled my nose, swirling memories to the surface. Each thrust felt like one from the past. All the times he had held me against a wall just like this. The times he devoured me like I was all he needed to survive. All the times he whispered dirty things in my ear to make me come.

But it was my turn today. "I love you, Professor Hunter," I whispered into his ear.

I came at the same time as him, the warmth of him inside of me tipping me over the edge. I felt drunk as he continued to hold me against the wall. His hot breath on the side of my neck was the most comforting sensation in the world. I was intoxicated by him.

He lightly kissed the side of my neck once more before placing his forehead against mine. His eyes were closed and I took the time to breathe him in. His exhales were the only air I needed. With him still inside of me and him holding me up in his arms I felt so at peace. And calm. And whole. Except for a lingering pain on the side of my neck.

"You gave me a hickey, didn't you?" I tried not to smile too hard.

He slowly opened his eyes. "Recently you've been forgetting that you're mine. Now you'll remember."

I was never going to forget again.

CHAPTER 8

Monday - *James*

For just a few minutes it felt like we were back in time, making love in my apartment in Newark. I wasn't sure why, but I tried to dismiss the thought. I loved how we met. I loved how we started. But I knew better than anyone now that the past belonged in the past. Remembering it was great, but reliving it was a nightmare. I was happy where we were. Here. Today.

We weren't the same people anymore. Penny and I had been through so much together. Her forgetting about the last several years had nearly killed me.

Seeing her crying on the bathroom floor made me forget about the past few weeks. I had made her feel like she had broken us. And that wasn't true at all. If anything, I loved her more than ever now. Losing her for a few weeks was the worst thing that had ever happened to me. Now I had her back. I didn't need her apologies. I just needed her.

When she came out of the bathroom adjusting her shirt, she almost looked bashful. I knew she was remembering. I just didn't know which parts she remembered.

"Hey," she said as she ran her fingers through her hair, trying to pull out a few knots.

I loved her unruly curls. She usually styled it now, but I liked it like this best. Natural. She didn't need anything added to her to look beautiful.

I walked over to her, grabbed both sides of her face, and placed my lips against hers. I felt her melt into me, and it pulled on my heartstrings. She was finally where she belonged again. "Hey yourself."

Penny laughed as she pulled away. But her eyes weren't dancing with humor. "You said things with your mom have changed?" She glanced over my shoulder at the closed door. "I still have an unsettled feeling in my stomach when I think about her."

"I think maybe she's acted the way she has because she felt threatened by you in my life."

"By me? Why?"

"Because you became everything to me so quickly. Nothing else mattered but you."

Her eyes locked with mine. "But that's not true anymore. You have your friends and family. Our family." She pressed her lips together. "I need to go see Liam. I need to hold him. I need to tell him I love him."

"He knows." I placed a gentle kiss against her forehead. "Visiting hours are over, but I'm sure we can convince someone to let us up."

"You've always been very good at that. I remember when you visited me after I got my concussion."

"Hmm." I brushed a loose strand of hair away from her face. "I didn't realize how important our memories were until you lost them. What else do you remember?"

"Besides the fact that you like to bribe nurses and that your mother hates me? Well…" her eyes dropped to my mouth. "Other things too. Lots of things." She bit down on her bottom lip.

"What don't you remember?" I tried not to stare at her lips, or else we'd wind up repeating our time in the shower. And Rob and my mother were waiting. We had already taken awhile in here. They were probably wondering if we were okay.

"I don't remember that day...when I went into the hospital." She placed her hand on her stomach.

"Nothing at all about it?" I wanted her to remember everything. But maybe it was better that she didn't remember that day. I hadn't been there for her when she needed me. I didn't want that seared into her brain when our relationship was still so fragile.

"No. And there are other holes too. Where my memories kind of...jump ahead I think. Almost like they're on fast-forward. I still want to read the rest of what I wrote. It might help."

"Just the important stuff."

She smiled.

"If everything comes back to you except the day of the accident, I think that might be for the best."

Her eyes locked with mine. "You're probably right. One advantage of losing your memory is that you don't have to remember the bad stuff." She took a deep breath. "Speaking of bad stuff...we should probably get this thing with your mom over with before I lose my nerve."

"She's actually hoping to come see Liam with us tonight. And Scarlett. I think she's finally ready to be a grandmother."

"She hasn't met either of them yet?" Penny touched the side of her forehead. "I guess I'm missing more than I realized."

"It's going to be fine. I promise. And if you feel at all uncomfortable with her seeing the children, I'll tell her she can't come. Okay?"

"Okay." She looked so adorably nervous. There was a vulnerability there that I wasn't used to seeing in her. Again, it made me feel like we were back in time. Back where we began. I needed to make sure I wasn't overwhelming her. I needed to make sure she felt safe with me.

I laced my fingers with hers and guided her out in the hall before she could change her mind. I was as nervous as her. My mom had agreed to apologize years ago, but an apology had never happened. She had been horrible to us before our wedding. Hell, she had been horrible to me my whole life. I felt that same sour feeling Penny did in her stomach. But I was sick of holding grudges. I was getting too old to harbor feelings of resentment toward my mother. I needed to let this go. My cardiologist would thank me later for being less stressed.

I was surprised to hear Rob's laughter filtering through the hall. Apparently my mother was making nice with him as well.

"Penny. Darling," my mom said as we entered the room. She stood up and approached us.

Penny was squeezing my hand so tightly it felt like she was going to cut off circulation to my fingers.

"I have so much I need to say to you," my mother said. "I wanted to protect my son. And in doing so, I realize that I wasn't really taking his opinions into consideration. I dismissed you as a young hussy with fluff for brains and never took the time to get to know you. Partially because of your family's status and partially because I adored Isabella so."

I couldn't believe when she stopped talking and stared at Penny expectantly. "That wasn't a good apology," I said before Penny could even reply. "You have to admit that you were wrong about her and her family."

"But her family is of unequal footing as…"

"Penny has half of everything I own." I pulled my hand out of hers. "She's better off than you now."

Rob laughed from the loveseat behind her.

My mother cleared her throat. "Clearly I wasn't calling her a poor hussy *now*. The idea that she changed by being around you was implied."

"Geez, Susan, come on," Rob said with a laugh and stood up to join the conversation. "You basically just insinuated that she used to be a hussy."

"For the last time, Robert, do not call me by my first name. I am your mother."

"You haven't been acting like it," he mumbled.

She sighed and turned back to me. "I've apologized to you and your brother. And your wife, James. I don't know what else you want from me. Anyone who marries into wealth understands common associations with doing such a thing. Where do you think the term gold digger came from?"

"We're leaving," I said.

Penny grabbed my arm. "No, it's okay. Honestly, she's right. Not about the hussy thing, obviously. And I don't love that insinuation. But it's hard marrying someone who has so much. I've certainly felt like I didn't belong more times than I can count. And she wasn't calling me a gold digger. She was simply using it as an example. Right, Mrs. Hunter?"

My mother smiled. "See. She understands my apology."

"I understand where you're coming from. But technically you haven't uttered the words 'I'm sorry.' And I for one would really appreciate hearing them."

Her words made me stand up a little taller. Sometimes I forgot that Penny didn't always need my protection. She could fend for herself. She was strong and brave. I was in awe of her.

Rob clapped our mom on the back as he walked over to Penny. He folded his arms across his chest as he stood beside us. Three against one. A united front. I was glad he was here. I'd never be able to accept my mother's apology until she apologized to him too. This was about all of us. Not just me and Penny.

"For heaven's sake. I'm sorry, Rob. I'm sorry, James. I'm sorry, Penny. Truly. I am." She sounded sincere.

I looked down at Penny. This was up to her. She was the most important person in my life. It was crucial that she and my mom both knew it.

She smiled up to me, definitely less nervous than before. "If your sons forgive you, I forgive you," she said and glanced at Rob too.

Rob winked at her. "Sure," he said. "But I'm still calling you Susan until Daphne agrees that you can be part of our lives too. It's not just about me anymore. I have a whole family that you haven't wanted to be a part of."

Our mother sighed. "Fine. Don't call me mom. But maybe my grandkids can call me grandma?" She looked at all of us hopefully.

I wrapped my arm around Penny's back. She nodded up at me with a smile on her face. For a few days, I thought my family was falling apart. Now we were more whole than ever. I looked back at my mother. "Okay, Grandma. Ready to meet them?"

CHAPTER 9
Monday - *Penny*

I had memories of James being closed off. Hard to read. Moody. But he wasn't like those memories. His heart was so big. He'd forgiven his mother. And I know I had said the same words, but I was still watching her suspiciously. She could say all the rude things or nice things in the world to me. But all that mattered to me was how she treated my husband. And Rob. Rob was one of my best friends. I wanted to protect him just as much as I wanted to protect James from pain. Maybe it was the momma bear in me.

I bit the inside of my lip. I hoped I really was a good mother. I hoped that this time when I saw my son I remembered him, instead of just meeting him for the first time. I'd know him now, right? I'd remember?

The elevator dinged open. I don't know what James had to do to get all of us up here. But any amount of money would be worth this moment. I stopped outside the NICU window and stared inside. I knew I had technically already met him once. But that wasn't me. That person was a ghost, a shell of who I really was. She hadn't known James. She wasn't whole. A shadow of what could have been if I hadn't run into James in that coffee shop so many years ago.

My train of thought halted when my eyes landed on my son. It felt like my heart ripped in half. I rushed to the door and pulled it open.

"Mrs. Hunter…"

I pressed my hand against the glass that was surrounding Liam. "I need to hold him."

"He's sleeping, Mrs. Hunter. I think…"

"Please let me hold him." My voice cracked. God, he was so small.

"Penny, he's getting stronger every day," James said.

I barely even heard him. I felt his hand on my shoulder, but I didn't really feel it. All I could feel was this shadow cross my soul.

"Please." I blinked back my tears. "I need to hold him." *I need to say hello before I miss the chance.* "Please."

"Alright, one second." The nurse stopped protesting and started maneuvering all the tubes attached to Liam.

As soon as he was in my arms, my tears started flowing freely. He felt like home in my arms. Like a piece of my soul was staring back at me. "Hey, baby boy."

His eyes stayed closed. I knew he was sleeping. I knew that, but for some reason, his closed eyes overwhelmed me. *Open your eyes. Open your eyes for me, Liam.* It was like I could feel him slipping away from me. I watched as my tears fell, staining his cheeks. And he still didn't move. He was so still and it terrified me. *Open your eyes. Please.*

James wrapped his arms around me from behind, holding me steady. I had fixed things with him. Miraculously, he had forgiven me for everything. But I couldn't fix this. I didn't know how to heal my son.

"What are we going to do?" I whispered. I wasn't even sure if James heard me. But then he kissed the side of my neck.

"We're going to wait." His breath was hot in my ear, giving me a sense of comfort. "And pray. And be with him as much as possible."

"But you're not religious."

"Praying to a God you didn't think you believed in during a crisis sometimes makes a believer out of the most hardened of souls. It makes you hope that miracles can happen."

I sniffed, trying to stop my tears. "Did you read that somewhere?" It was beautiful.

"No, it's just…true."

I turned my head to look up at him.

He reached out and gently wiped away my tears. "God, if you're out there, please heal our son," he said. "Please watch over him. Let us bring him home."

Whatever tears he had wiped away started falling freely again.

"And let Penny's memories keep coming back. Let her heal."

"And let James heal too," I added. I still needed to talk to him about what exactly had happened to him. But it was true, praying to a God we didn't necessarily believe in couldn't possibly hurt. "Amen?"

"Amen," James confirmed.

Liam kicked one of his feet out and my tears were replaced with a smile. I definitely remembered him kicking me. A lot. It had been his favorite hobby. But the kick didn't seem as strong as it had in my stomach.

"Can I hold him?" Susan asked.

I instinctively hugged Liam tighter to my chest. I didn't want to let him go. It felt like he was exactly where he belonged. I couldn't even imagine having to leave him tonight.

Susan put her arms out to take him.

She was trying. I knew that. She wanted to be a part of Liam's life. Whatever that may entail. I leaned down and kissed his forehead. "I love you, baby boy. You're going to come home soon. I promise." It didn't matter if my promise was empty. That's what parents did, right? Fight for their children? And I'd do anything to make my promise true. Anything. I reluctantly placed Liam into Susan's arms.

I felt empty as soon as he was gone. Like a part of me was missing. I turned and pressed the side of my face against James' chest. He held me as I cried. His hand running up and down my back was the most comforting thing in the world. And the smell of his cologne. And the softness of his t-shirt. I remembered all of it.

"It's going to be okay," he said.

He was the heart of our family. And I'd take his lies any day. I liked that he sheltered me from pain. I loved him for it. But he couldn't protect me from this, no matter how much I wished that he could. We were going to face all this together. As a team.

"It's late," James said. "We can come back in the morning with Scarlett."

"She never goes to sleep without a bedtime story." The words tumbled out of my mouth and I knew that they were true. "She's probably giving everyone back home trouble."

"Most likely." He smiled down at me. "She's going to be excited to see you."

"Not that imposter in my place? She could tell. She knew something wasn't right."

"She's a smart kid."

"Like her father."

James shook his head. "Like her mother."

"Hey, J.J. How are you tonight?" Rob asked.

I glanced over at Rob. He was bouncing up and down, holding Liam close to his chest.

"J.J.?" I asked.

"It's my nickname for him," Rob said. "You shoulda named him James Junior in my opinion."

"I love the name Liam." I looked up at James. "I can't believe you named him that though. I thought you didn't like it."

"I never said I didn't like Liam. I just thought it was going to be a girl."

I smiled, remembering a simpler time. When betting on the sex of our child was our only concern. But Liam was perfect. He was just small. "How is he doing?" I asked the nurse on duty.

"His doctor will be in tomorrow morning if you want updates."

I swallowed hard. Her response wasn't exactly settling. "That would be great. What time?"

"Let me go check the schedule for you."

"It's okay," James said as he slipped his arm around me. "We'll be here for most of the day. We won't miss him."

"Alright. I'll see you both tomorrow then." She gave us a kind smile as she went to put Liam back down.

"Just one second," I said and pulled him into my arms once more. It still felt like I was running out of time even now that I saw him. It was the worst feeling in the world. "I remember you, Liam. I remember you and I'm here to fight for you now. So don't you forget that. Okay?" He was still sleeping, his chest rising and falling quickly, like he was struggling for air, which I knew he was.

Liam kicked one of his feet out again and I smiled. He and I had an agreement. When he kicked, that meant we were on the same page. I looked down at him and tried to ingrain his adorable little face into my mind. I wasn't sure how many of these moments we'd have. And once you lost your memories, you started to appreciate them even more. Especially the important ones. The ones that were fleeting.

***

Coming home earlier tonight had been jarring. Too many faces. Too much noise. All I needed was James and he hadn't been there. I had probably been rude and insensitive. God, they had all thought I had run off with Tyler. It was a freaking mess.

But when we walked into our home now, there was no longer a search party. The silence was startling. I was expecting Scarlett to run into the foyer and jump into my arms, knowing it was truly me again. I'd twirl her around in excitement. But I guess I had built up our reuniting in my head.

James locked the door behind us. Rob and Susan had gone home after the hospital visit. It was late. And I needed my moment with Scarlett before I introduced her to a stranger anyway. She had been practically living with one as it was.

"Why is the freezer door open?" James asked.

I laughed as we entered the kitchen. "How should I know? I wasn't here either."

He frowned and closed it. There were small little brown dots on the kitchen floor too. He bent down for a closer look. "Chocolate? Maybe?" He raised his left eyebrow at me.

I laughed and looked toward the stairs where the chocolaty trail led. "Nothing to put a child to sleep like chocolate ice cream. I was worried that Scar liked Melissa more than me. And no wonder…she feeds her ice cream as a late night snack. How can I possibly compete with that?"

"Scarlett loves you, baby. How about we go let her know that you're home. She's probably still awake if she just ate ice cream anyway."

"True." I gripped James' hand tightly as we walked up the stairs together. I had been so worried about remembering that I hadn't thought about what Scarlett remembered. What if she didn't recognize the real me? What if she preferred my 19-year-old mind more? Was that possible?

Melissa and Josh were sleeping on the floor. Her head was in his lap, and Scarlett's favorite book, *The Ruin of House Hornbolt*, was on the floor by Josh's hand, like he had dropped it as he dozed off. Melissa always wore a lot of makeup, but whatever was on her face right now was definitely overboard. And completely horrible. Her lipstick was basically all over her face. The eyeshadow had also left her eyelids. Josh's hair had been pulled into two pigtails that could really only be described as horns with bows. I stifled a laugh. They looked absolutely ridiculous.

"I put Aunt Melissa and Uncle Josh to sleep for you," Scarlett said. "They were hard to put down."

I pulled my eyes away from the sleeping couple to see Scarlett sitting in her bed eating a huge bowl of ice cream. Well, technically it wasn't even a bowl. It was a saucepan, which was one of the only cabinets she could get into without finding a way to crawl up onto the counter. She was holding the handle in one hand and a huge spoon used for stirring things on the stove in the other. The saucepan was balancing precariously on one knee.

"Scar, what are you doing?" I asked. "You're not allowed to eat ice cream before bed and you know it."

"But they said it was okay and that I could have as much as I wanted." She pulled the saucepan tightly to her chest. "I didn't do anything bad."

"And what have we said about lying?"

"Well, *that's* bad. But I didn't do that. I'm always a good girl." She looked down at her ice cream and then back up at me. A smile broke over her face. "Lying's bad! My mommy told me it was bad! Only my real mommy knows about lying rules!" She launched herself out of her bed, knocking the saucepan onto her comforter. I didn't even care that she had made a mess. All I cared about was her. I knelt down to catch her in my arms.

"Mommy." She started to cry, her little body shaking against mine.

I clutched her even tighter. "It's okay, Scar. I'm back. And I'm not going anywhere ever again."

"I didn't think you'd ever come back. I thought you left me."

"No, no, baby girl." I kissed the top of her head. "I'd never leave you."

"But you did. You left me and Daddy and Liam. You left us. Why'd you leave us? Was it something I did wrong? Because I'm sorry."

"No. You didn't do anything wrong." God, I hated that she thought any of this was her fault. How could I fix this? I looked up at James.

He was quickly wiping under his eyes. He turned away from me when he noticed I was staring. My heart felt like it was cracking into pieces. I had hurt both of them so much.

"I'm the one that's sorry," I said. "I got hurt. I couldn't remember. And I'm so so sorry."

"But it's all my fault. I tried to tell you about the snapes and no one believed me." She was sobbing now, soaking my shirt in tears and snot, but I didn't care in the slightest. "It's my fault the snapes got you."

"No, no, no. Shhhh." I ran my hand up and down her back. "None of this was your fault. Don't think that for a second. You can't control other people's intentions, sweetie."

"What is intentions?" She sniffled loudly.

"It means…plans. That doctor had plans that weren't nice. But none of that was your fault. And he's locked up now. He'll never hurt us again. I promise."

"And you'll never leave again?"

"I'll never leave you again, Scar. Never."

She pulled away and put her hands on both sides of my face. She stared into my eyes like she could read my soul. And then she nodded. "Only *my* mommy looks at me like that."

I was trying not to cry. "Like what, Scar?"

"Like…like I'm never bad."

Oh, sweetie. I pulled her back into a hug.

I glanced up at James again. He had quickly composed himself. For the first time tonight, I realized how tired he looked.

"We should get to bed, Scar," I said.

She wrapped her arms tighter around my neck. "I want to sleep with you and Daddy."

James nodded with a smile. "You two go get ready for bed. I'll clean all this up. And you're going to need this." He leaned down and picked up Scarlett's favorite book.

CHAPTER 10

Monday - *James*

I put the saucepan onto the drying rack and turned off the water. I was exhausted. If I sat down on the kitchen floor right now, I was pretty sure I'd fall asleep. And I'd wake up with pigtails and makeup all over my face like poor Melissa and Josh. I didn't have the heart to wake them up. I had just covered them with a blanket and left them on the floor of Scarlett's bedroom. They looked as exhausted as I felt.

I ran my hand down my face. I hadn't expected to feel so much emotion when Scarlett jumped into Penny's arms. Clearly I needed to pull myself together. Or maybe I just needed sleep. Penny needed me to be strong right now. Falling apart wasn't an option. But all I wanted to do was hold Penny as tightly as I could. And thank her for coming back. And beg her to never leave again. My daughter wasn't the only one that depended on Penny. Honestly, I probably depended on her even more than my child. I needed her like the air I breathed. I sighed and tossed the dry towel on top of the saucepan. It could wait until morning. Right now, I just needed to fall asleep with my arms wrapped around my beautiful wife.

When I reached our bedroom, I stopped and leaned against the doorjamb. Penny was running her fingers through Scarlett's hair and reading. For a moment, I just stared at the two of them.

Penny turned the page of the book and continued to read aloud, oblivious of my watching.

"Two gold drachmas for the beautiful lady," said the vendor with a crooked yellow smile.

Oriana immediately shook her head and took a step back. "I'm just looking."

"Nonsense, the color matches your golden hair." He smiled again.

She looked back down at the fabric. Maybe she could use it to patch the tear. A few designs sewn into the dress might be just what it needed. She ran her fingers across the smooth silk. The way it caught the sun truly was gorgeous. How could Prince Rixin's gaze not fall on her in something so lovely? But would it be enough fabric to cover the tear? She had planned to sew a whole new dress, so she hadn't measured it. And this wasn't nearly enough fabric for an entire dress. Oriana thought about the plain dresses that most of the women wore in the castle. Having a design would help her stand out. Or would it look foolish since no one else was wearing such a thing?

"Two gold is a good deal," said the merchant. "Usually I'd charge twice that, but I have a soft spot for women with blue eyes."

She thought of the three gold drachmas sitting in her coin purse. It was meant for a whole spool of fabric, not just a swatch.

"Get back here!" a deep voice boomed from a nearby merchant stand.

Oriana turned her head just in time to see a dirty little squirrel, with what appeared to be a vine of grapes in his mouth, scurrying toward her. It dashed across the fabric merchant's table like a miniature sandstorm. One second it was crawling up a spool, then the next it was jumping onto a pile of fabric. The fabric teetered and fell onto the dusty ground. The merchant grabbed for the rodent, but he ended up with only a fistful of air. Oriana screamed and stepped back, tossing the swatch back onto the table. And then, just as quickly as it had come, the squirrel leapt onto a carpet on the side of the booth and disappeared onto the makeshift roof over the next vendor's table.

"Your pet just ruined everything!" yelled the fabric merchant, waving a dagger in the air.

"My pet? I've never seen that creature before in my life." Oriana looked around at the mess. Pieces of fabric were strewn in the dirt. Tiny brown footprints dotted the cloth left off the table. And the carpet now featured little tears where the squirrel's claws had dug into it on its way up to the roof. Oriana started to walk away, but the vendor grabbed her wrist.

"You have to pay for that," he snarled.

"Let go of me." She tried to pull her arm away, but the merchant tightened his grip.

"Two hundred gold for the lot of it."

"But it wasn't my fault."

"That animal of yours ruined everything. This is my livelihood!" He yanked her back toward the table.

Fear gripped her heart. Three gold was all she had. Why had she ventured out alone? "I only have three."

"That one swatch alone was worth twice that."

"I don't have the money, but I can get it. If you just let me go to the castle..."

"The castle?" he practically screamed. "You're not going anywhere until I get what I'm due." He pushed her against the table. "If I can't have it in gold, I'll take it in flesh."

She knew the punishment for stealing. But she hadn't stolen anything. Why was everyone just watching this? Why was no one standing up for her? She knew in her heart that Arwin wouldn't let anything happen to her. He was fair and just. But her belief waned as the vendor gripped the dagger tighter in his hand.

A whistling sound pierced the air. She turned to see who had produced the shrill noise. Was it a guard coming to stop this madness?

Before she could locate the source of the whistle, the fabric merchant started screaming behind her. But this time it wasn't directed at her. She turned back to see the squirrel had returned, dangling by its mouth from the merchant's ear.

A strong hand slipped into Oriana's. "Hurry, this way," said the stranger's deep voice. Before she could even turn to look at the man, he had already pulled her into the crowd away from the fabric merchant.

"I'm not going anywhere with a complete stranger," she hissed. And certainly not a strange man! It wouldn't be proper. She pulled her hand away.

He turned to face her. He had a smile and dimples worthy of any royalty. "Are you trying to get yourself killed?" He backed away from her, slowly disappearing into the masses of patrons.

Of course I'm not trying to get myself killed! Especially for a crime she didn't commit. Arwin must have sent this man to save her. She took a step toward him. He winked and took off in the opposite direction, as if he'd known she'd follow him all along.

The nerve of him. But she didn't have time to overthink her decision. She needed to get away from the fabric merchant. She quickened her pace as she caught up to the only man offering her any help.

"This way." The stranger grabbed her hand again as the two of them ducked beneath a weathered canopy. He may have had the face of a prince, but she knew he was not one. His hands were rough and calloused from years of labor. And his clothes were torn and dirty. She shook away the thought, not knowing why she was analyzing him when she should be focused solely on escaping.

"Stop them!" yelled the fabric merchant from somewhere far behind them.

The stranger pulled Oriana down a side street, away from the market. He kicked open a door and she followed him in just as the merchant tore around the corner.

"That way!" yelled the merchant. He had amassed an angry mob.

Oriana struggled to keep pace as the stranger dashed up a flight of stairs two at a time. They burst through another door onto the roof of the building. He dropped her hand and jumped across a gap to another roof.

Her feet skidded to a stop.

"You have to jump!" he called to her.

She heard the merchant's voice again. He seemed even closer. Oh bother. She grabbed the hem of her skirt and lifted it to her knees. With a deep breath, she took a step back and then ran as fast as she could. She leapt across the small divide. Her momentum made her stumble to her knees as she landed.

The stranger pulled her to her feet before she had a chance to recover. They burst through another door and ran down the stairs. The thick sheets over the windows rendered the room almost completely dark.

"This'll do." He caught her arm and pulled her into the corner of the room.

Oriana started to protest, but the stranger pressed his finger against her lips. "Shh," he whispered into her ear.

She swallowed hard as she looked up at him. Her heart seemed to skip a beat. Yes, a face worthy of a prince indeed. Although, no prince she had ever imagined would dare find himself in such a situation.

His finger fell from her lips but his body stayed pressed against hers.

"I should probably..." she tried to duck away from his arms.

"Just one moment," he whispered. The warmth of his breath against her ear sent a shiver down her spine.

Suddenly it sounded like a herd of rhinos was stampeding across the roof. She threw her arms around his neck and didn't protest at all when he held her firmly against his chest. She didn't want to imagine what the fabric merchant would do if he caught her. What had she gotten herself into?

"Shh," he whispered again. The words and warmth comforted her slightly.

IVY SMOAK

As the silence settled around them once again, the stranger took a step back from her. "Are you alright, m'lady?"

"Yes. I'm fine." A little bruised and scraped, but nothing lasting. "And you?"

He laughed. "I've been through worse."

Her eyes slowly began to focus in the dark. She couldn't seem to stop staring at his disarming features.

A smile spread across his face as he watched her.

"What's your name?" she asked.

"Bastian." He took her hand and brought it to his lips. "It's a pleasure to make your acquaintance." He placed a gentle kiss on her hand.

The gesture sent a chill down her spine.

A squeaking noise made them both turn their heads. The same squirrel from the market scampered down the stairs toward them. Oriana squealed and took a step back, slipping on an uneven patch of floor.

Bastian easily caught her with one arm.

She momentarily lost her breath as her hands wrapped around his biceps.

Bastian laughed as he held her body against his. "It's quite alright. It's just Nut."

It only took Oriana a moment to realize that she was clinging to a man she didn't even know. She immediately took a step back. "Nut? It has a name?"

"Of course he has a name." Bastian squatted down and held his hand out toward the squirrel. "Don't you, boy?" The squirrel jumped up onto his shoulder.

"That...that animal almost got me killed!"

Bastian patted the squirrel's head as he stood up. "He also saved you." Bastian pulled a grape out of his pocket and handed it to the squirrel. Nut grabbed it with his greedy little paws and nibbled away at the outside of the grape.

"I wouldn't have needed saving if...wait a second. You made that rodent attack."

Nut stopped nibbling mid-bite.

"Rodent?" Bastian said. "That's a little harsh. Although he is in desperate need of a good bath."

Nut threw the remaining piece of grape at Bastian's cheek.

Bastian laughed. "You know I'm just kidding with you," he said and patted the squirrel's head again. "Besides, Nut's distraction also allowed me to get you this." He pulled out the golden fabric that the merchant had been trying to sell her.

"But I...I didn't pay for that."

Bastian winked. "It can be our little secret." He pushed the fabric into her hands. "It really does match your hair perfectly."

The dark room suddenly felt stifling. Their eyes locked. No one had ever looked at Oriana the way Bastian was staring at her. It made her heart race. And her palms felt sweaty. This was how she desired for Rixin to look at her.

"I should probably get back," Oriana said. She pressed her lips together, wondering why she had broken the spell. Bastian was making her incredibly nervous.

He took a step back from her, pushed a tattered curtain to the side, and looked out the window.

Oriana smoothed out her skirt while his eyes weren't trained on her.

"It appears everything has settled down. You should be safe to go." He turned back toward her and gave her another charming smile.

"I don't know how to thank you." She looked down at the cloth in her hands, unsure whether a thank you truly was in order. He was a thief. A thief who had saved her life. With a smile that could light up this dark room.

"No need to thank me. It was my pleasure, my lady." He winked again and jumped onto the window sill.

"But..." began Oriana. *But before she could say another word, he was gone.*

The push and pull in Scarlett's favorite story reminded me of my relationship with Penny. In our case though, it truly felt like she had saved me. Not the other way around. I smiled as I watched the two of them. The two women in my life that had saved me from the hell I had been living.

Penny was great at reading to Scarlett. She changed her voices depending on the characters, which always made Scarlett giggle. But tonight, it had just put Scarlett fast asleep.

"You're better at that than I am," I said.

She looked up. "At reading? I highly doubt that." She closed the book but still continued to stroke Scarlett's hair.

"At reading out loud. The voices you make."

For a moment she looked embarrassed. "What, you like my suave thief voice?" she said deeply.

I laughed. "Not as much as your princess voice."

She smiled. "Well that's good. Or else I'd be worried about what kind of kinky things you were into."

"Nothing quite that kinky." I walked into the room and pulled my shirt off over my head. I forced myself not to smile when I caught her staring at me undressing. Such a simple act seemed so normal a few weeks ago. And now there was a new-ness to it. She wasn't used to seeing me like this. It would take time for us to find our normal routine again. Time for us to re-member what normalcy even felt like. I was okay with that. I paused before pulling off my jeans. If there was even a part of her that still wanted to take things slowly, I wanted to respect that. Even if we had already sped things up quite a bit earlier to-night.

I grabbed a pair of pajama pants from the closet and gestured to the bathroom. "I'm going to finish getting ready for bed. Feel free to keep reading if you'd like."

She didn't look up at me. Instead, she buried her face in the book. And a few minutes later when I reemerged her body was curled around Scarlett's and her eyes were tightly closed. I wasn't sure if she was trying to look like she was asleep or if she was just so happy to be back in Scarlett's good graces.

I climbed into bed, trying not to disturb her. It had been a long day for both of us. I understood if she didn't want to talk anymore. But as soon as the covers shifted she opened her beautiful blue eyes. "I really am sorry, James. For everything."

I stared down at the two of them. A smile was stretched across Scarlett's face, but my dear wife looked full of apprehension.

"Baby, how many times do I have to tell you that you have nothing to be sorry for." I reached out to tuck a loose strand of hair behind her ear and her face melted into my touch.

"When I couldn't remember our past, it felt like a bolt of electricity shocked me every time we touched," she said. "Like my body was trying to tell me how perfect we were together."

I smiled. "And you don't feel it any longer?"

"No, I do." Her cheeks were rosy, like she was embarrassed by her admission. "But it's different. Familiar, I guess I mean. In a good way."

In a good way. "I still feel it too." I rested my head down on my pillow. "Like my body is the negative end of a magnet and you're the positive end."

"Why do you always do that? Make yourself the bad part of an equation?"

"There's no bad part of a magnet." She was right though. I automatically made myself the negative end. Why did I do that?

Penny just stared at me.

"I don't know why I do it," I said.

"I've never met a better man in my entire life. There's no reason on earth that you of all people should be self-deprecating, James. You're perfect."

I laughed at that. "Hardly. You should have seen your face when I told you I was an addict."

"Which time?"

"The second one. You were much kinder the first time I told you."

"I remember the first time. It was raining. Our relationship had felt so strained. Because you were hiding a part of your past from me. But your past doesn't define you, James. You can be perfect even if you've had a hard life. The difference between that time and this time was that I loved you then. And when you told me the second time you were a stranger. It's easier to judge a stranger when you don't know how pure their heart is."

"I didn't know that you never told anyone. About my problems. Melissa didn't know. I just assumed that she did."

"It wasn't my place to tell anyone. It's your story to share with whomever you choose. Not mine."

"It wasn't because you were embarrassed by me?"

"James." She removed her arms from around Scarlett. "How could you even think that?" She climbed over Scarlett's sleeping body and then over me to try to close the distance between us.

I resisted grabbing her hips and pulling her on top of me. Our daughter was sleeping peacefully beside us. I didn't want to disrupt her sleep, no matter how badly my body was calling for Penny's.

She fell onto the other side of me with a quiet "oomph" before nestling herself between my arms. "Never in my life have I been embarrassed by you. I've always been the embarrassing one. I'm from a lower class," she said in an accent that sounded far too similar to my mother's.

I laughed. "I've never been embarrassed by you. I love you. I've loved you since the first moment we met and you took my breath away."

"And I love you." She yawned and closed her eyes, like the only thing keeping her from sleep before was the lack of my arms around her. "We were both wrong, you know," she said into my chest with another yawn. "Love isn't light or dark or a whirlwind of color."

"If it isn't those things, then how would you describe it?" I pulled her a little closer to my chest, savoring the feeling of her breath against my skin.

"This." She sighed like she had never been more content in her entire life. "This is love."

She fell asleep in my arms, her breath slowly becoming more shallow. I wanted to stay up forever watching her. For a few weeks I didn't know if I'd ever be able to have another one of these moments. And now that it was here, I was terrified it would slip away again.

I stared at her luscious lips and the delicate curve of her jaw. Her long eyelashes cast shadows on her cheeks. And her red hair shimmered even without a light source. She was perfection in every sense of the word.

Her chest slowly rose and fell, outlining her perfect breasts through one of my old t-shirts. It was the sexiest thing I had ever seen. She moaned in her sleep, a sound I was all too familiar with when I was deep inside of her. I bit back a groan of my own. If my daughter wasn't asleep behind me, I'd wake up Penny and make love to her. Again and again until neither one of us had enough energy to continue.

All I wanted to do was catch up on lost time between us. I wanted to show her how much I loved her. Penny was right. Love couldn't really be defined. It wasn't a balance of light and darkness or a whirlwind of color. It was a feeling. This feeling. And I'd spend the rest of my life making sure she felt this too.

CHAPTER 11

Tuesday - *Penny*

I wasn't sure when I drifted to sleep, but when I opened my eyes I almost screamed. Then everything came back in a rush. It was James' arms wrapped tightly around me. My husband. *I'm in New York City. I'm a mother. I'm a wife.* I took a deep breath. My heartbeat kicked up a notch instead of calming down. It all still felt unfamiliar, even though it felt like home. Would that feeling go away? Would this ever become normal again?

There was no light streaming into the room. It was probably the middle of the night. But my eyes slowly adjusted to the darkness as I stared at the man lying next to me. He belonged in a magazine. Or on a T.V. show. *How did he end up here with me in the city that never sleeps?* He belonged in Hollywood.

He said he had forgiven me. He said he loved me. He had said all the right things. But was any of it true? Were we really happy? I couldn't remember anything about the day of the accident. But I did remember the note that I found. The one where it sounded like I tried to take my own life. James mentioned tonight that it was better if I didn't remember that day. Was that why?

I stared at the stubble along his jaw line and the slope of his nose. His muscular shoulders and strong chest. I gently placed my hand on his left peck and ran my thumb along the scar. He said it was a minor cardiac episode. He brushed it off as no big deal. But he had surgery. Doctors had cut him open and done something to fix him. Or they had tried to fix him. James' exhales sounded slightly labored. Like it was hard for him to breathe. He was more hurt than he was letting on. That much was clear. He was focused on me remembering and Liam healing and wasn't thinking of himself. I felt fine. I was fine. Liam and James were the ones that needed my help, not the other way around.

All I knew for sure was that the man in front of me had my heart. He still felt like a stranger in some ways. But my memories were coming back. I knew that I loved him more than life itself. So I was going to figure out a way to alleviate any stress on him. And find a way to heal him and my baby. I leaned forward and placed a kiss against his scar. When I did, my eyes landed on a tattoo on the side of his ribcage. I had seen a glimpse of it before, but now the whole thing was visible in front of me.

It looked like the lines of an EKG. The ones you see on heart monitors. The beginning of it was flat and there was a date on it, and then the lines started up and down. It was the date when we first met in the coffee shop. His words came back to me in a rush. "My life began the day I met you," I whispered out loud. But there were two more dates beneath the first one now. The date that Scarlett was born. And the date that Liam was born. Tears pricked the corners of my eyes. His heart beat for us. His family. Another memory rushed to the surface. One where James was hurt. Where he needed me just as much as he needed me now.

I woke up in the middle of the night freezing cold. I was hunched over in the chair beside James' bed, curled up in a ball. My eyes blinked in the darkness. The only light in the room was the medical equipment and the moon shining in through the windows.

I felt like I needed to throw up again. But I didn't have anything left to throw up. I was going to be a bad mother. Because I was selfish. Because I didn't know how to live without James. And every day that passed it seemed more likely that I'd need to.

The beeping was all I could hear in the room. The constant beeping. The beeping that was slowly driving me insane.

I wrapped my arms around myself and stood up. Despite how cold I felt, that wasn't why I had woken up. I was dreaming of our wedding night and what could have been. I let a small smile unfold on my lips. I pictured his hands on me, whispering that I was his wife. And he had let me slowly take off his tie and tuxedo jacket. I had unbuttoned his shirt and found his tattoo. His wedding present. The present I had completely forgotten about.

I glanced at the door. No one was going to come in right now. I needed to find it. I needed to see his gift to me. I slowly climbed onto his bed and lay down beside him.

He didn't smell like James. He smelled like the cheap shaving cream they had let me shave his face with and the soap I sponged him with. I ran my fingers down the scruff that was already forming on his face again. I wanted to kiss him, but there was a tube down his throat. Instead I gently ran my index finger across his bottom lip.

"Wake up, James. Please. You promised you wouldn't leave me. You told me this love was forever and always."

Nothing.

Every time he didn't respond, it killed me a little more inside. I slowly pulled down the front of his hospital gown, revealing tons of wires attached to his chest, monitoring his heartbeat. The tattoo wasn't on his chest. I kept pulling.

First I saw the bandage on his ribcage. Where they had fixed his punctured lung. I gently kissed the bandage. Then I saw the larger bandage on his stomach, the evidence of his ruptured spleen. I gently kissed the second bandage. But there was no tattoo.

I had the strangest feeling that maybe this wasn't James. Maybe this was some imposter, and James was somewhere happy and healthy. Somewhere away from me. Somewhere where no one would try to hurt him. But I knew that wasn't true. I knew every contour of his six pack. I knew the line of his happy trail.

I tried to swallow down the lump in my throat as I pulled the gown down his arms. There was the bandage on his arm. Stitches. I should have been counting my blessings, not my husband's fatal wounds. All three, so close to his heart that it broke mine even more.

Again, there was no tattoo. Where was it? I moved his arm slightly and looked along the inside of his bicep. And that's when I saw it. On the side of his chest, hidden by his arm. Because it was personal. It was only for me to see. Because he was mine and I was his.

"James." I ran my finger up and down the pulse of the tattoo. "You promised me forever. Getting married was supposed to be our new beginning. Not the end." I was choking on my words. "It's too soon! You have to wake up. I need you. I need you!"

I splayed my hand on his chest. "Wake up! You have to wake up! I need you. Baby, please, I need you." I pressed the side of my head against his chest. I needed to hear his heartbeat. I needed to know he was going to be okay. "Please, James. You promised. Please don't leave me like this. Please don't leave us."

And that's when I saw it. His index finger moved.

I blinked back my tears. "I'm going to fix everything, James. I'm going to take care of our family," I whispered into the darkness. I slowly ducked out from between his arms and slid out of bed, being careful not to wake him. I looked over to see Scarlett sleeping peacefully. Every few breaths she made this adorable little snoring noise. I knew she hadn't been sleeping well with everything going on. She only ever snored when she was truly exhausted. She would probably be out for several more hours.

I glanced at the clock. It was only 4 in the morning. There was plenty of time to do all the research that I needed. I tiptoed out of the bedroom and down the hall. Melissa and Josh were still sleeping on Scarlett's bedroom floor. I glanced into Liam's empty room. *Always empty.* I remembered taking Scarlett to the paint store to pick out the color. She and James spent the whole day painting this room, getting it ready for him. James had insisted that I couldn't help, that I needed rest. But I watched the two of them laugh all day long, paint smeared on their clothes, hands, and faces. More paint ended up on them than it did on the walls. And I remembered thinking how lucky our baby was to join this family. A family full of love. And how soon I was going to get to bring him home. Tears pooled in the corners of my eyes. *I'm going to fix this.* I ignored the ache in my chest as I made my way down the stairs.

A memory flashed of a pool of blood at the bottom of the stairs and I froze mid-step. Rob had been hurt here. I remembered that feeling of despair seep over me. We had all been hurt here. It felt like everyone was always out to get us. So many people had tried to break us down. The University of New Castle. Isabella. James' mother. Dr. Nelson. We'd had our fair share of heartache and suffering. Enough was enough. I had always been a believer in fate. But fate had a funny way of returning the favor. *Pick on someone your own size, stupid fate!*

I walked down the rest of the stairs, pushing aside the negative memories. I only wanted to remember the positive ones. There were more of those. I could picture the Christmas garland strung around the banister and the tree in the living room on Christmas morning. A surprise from James even though he always tried to convince me it was actually Santa. He did it every year. Turned our home into a Christmas wonderland. Everywhere I turned, more memories rushed back. The good outweighed the bad tenfold. And I was going to put the bad to bed permanently this time.

When I reached my office another memory flooded to the surface. When we first moved in and this room was empty, James and I had made love in front of the fireplace. He had been complaining about not hiring movers and I had wanted to lighten his spirits. I wasn't sure who recommended the idea, but we had ended up playing hide-and-go-seek. He had scared me half to death when his arms wrapped around me in the darkness. A smile spread across my face. But he more than made up for the fright.

I collapsed in my desk chair and turned on my laptop. As soon as I opened up an internet browser I started typing away. I looked up poison and how important it was to pump your stomach. I wasn't sure if Liam or mine had been pumped. I looked up preemies and how their chances at survival depended on how far away from their due dates they were born. All the problems and issues they could have down the road. It was like I jumped into a dark hole and couldn't escape. I researched hospitals and experimental drugs and jotted notes down in a notebook the whole time. The odds weren't in our favor. I already knew that. But that didn't mean there wasn't hope. And I had to have hope. If I didn't have that, there was nothing to hold on to.

I turned to what I knew about James' condition. I learned about the different chambers of the heart, not knowing which of his was affected by his cardiac episode. Just the words cardiac episode were rather vague, not providing much help at all. But if he had surgery it was definitely more serious than he was letting on. I knew all about his stress levels and how they affected his

heart. He was supposed to be careful. And I couldn't help thinking that if I had been a little more careful, a little more aware of
my surroundings, none of this would have happened. I could
have prevented what happened to my son. I could have prevented what happened to James. I could have prevented all of this.

I tried to ignore the thought as I jotted down the name of the
best cardiologist in the United States. I had never cared about
James' money until this moment. We had all the best everything
at our disposal. There was no reason for us to stay here in New
York City if the best of the best wasn't here. And it wasn't. Not
for Liam or James. We'd either fly the doctors we needed out
here or go directly to them.

Only once my research for my husband and son was thor-
oughly exhausted did I start looking into my own problems. It
took me a while to figure out how to spell bilateral oophorectomy. And once I figured it out, I wish that I hadn't. The sadness I
had felt when I first found out was heightened even more now
that I knew what it was like to have children. I never wanted to
stop at two. I wanted three or four or more. I wiped the tears
away from underneath my eyes. It wasn't reversible. There wasn't
anything that anyone could do. Liam would be my last child. End
of story. And I wasn't sure if he'd live. I missed out on his first
few weeks. I missed out on his birth. I missed out on everything
and it was my last chance to experience it.

I took a deep breath. This wasn't about me. I hadn't wandered down here in the middle of the night to grieve what I had
lost. I came down here to fix whatever I could. But no matter
how hard I tried to bury down the pain, it wouldn't go away.
Tears kept spilling down my cheeks as I lifted up my phone and
dialed the number of the doctor I had found that had the highest
success rate with rehabilitating preemies. I needed to book flights,

car rentals, hotels. I had too much to do. There wasn't time to fall apart on the what-could-have-beens.

CHAPTER 12
Tuesday - *James*

I reached out and felt empty sheets. The familiar pain in my chest returned. Not from the surgery, but from the feeling of loss that had overcome me. I had been sleeping alone for weeks. And every morning I woke up reaching for Penny. Some mornings I wondered if this was how widowers always felt. Reaching out for a spouse that was no longer there. A ghost whose presence became less and less every day as their smell faded away. As their laughter became a distant memory. As the feeling of their lips grew harder to remember. As the memory of their smile disappeared from existence.

But then I heard a small snore from behind me. I opened my eyes and turned to see my daughter sleeping beside me. She was smiling in her sleep, hugging one of her stuffed animals tightly. And I remembered that I hadn't gone to sleep alone last night. Penny was back. She came back to me. And I didn't need to remember her smell, touch, taste, and sound. *She's home.* I slowly sat up and ran my hand down my face, trying to ease away the sleep and the bad memories. I had almost been swallowed whole by them. I had almost lost everything.

But Penny was definitely back. So where was she? I glanced at the clock. It was only 5:30 in the morning. My feeling of relief quickly disappeared. She promised she wouldn't leave again. I pushed the sheets off of me and practically tripped out of my bed. I glanced back to see Scarlett still sleeping peacefully before I jogged out of the room. I wanted to call for Penny, but I didn't want to wake anyone else sleeping.

She wasn't in Liam or Scarlett's room. I ran down the stairs. Penny wasn't in the kitchen or the living room. There were plenty of mornings when I found her on the couch with a cup of tea, a blanket, and a good book. But not this morning. It felt like my heart was going to beat out of my chest. She promised me she wouldn't leave again. I knew she was remembering. I could tell by the way she looked at me. The way she kissed me. Where the fuck was she?

I glanced into the dining room to find it empty before walking down the hall. I breathed a sigh of relief when I found her sitting in her office, her knees pulled up to her chest, balancing a cup of tea in one hand and moving her computer mouse around with the other. She didn't hear me or see me, she was completely engrossed in whatever she was doing on her laptop.

"Penny, what are you doing up so early?" My voice came out croaky and strange. I sounded desperate. I tried to swallow down the insecurities. She came home. She was still here. I took another deep breath and the pain in my chest eased.

Her eyes flitted to mine in the darkness. "I couldn't sleep." There was something alarming in her voice. Pain. Emotion. Fear. I was by her side in a second, putting my arms around her, hoping that they somehow helped ease her hurt.

"What happened? Is everything okay?"

She quickly wiped tears away from beneath her eyes. "It's nothing. I'm fine." But everything sounded wrong in her voice.

There was no way I was going to drop this. Not when our relationship was still so fragile. I wasn't going to let anything else break. "Baby, talk to me. Let me in."

"God, it's stupid." She angrily wiped her tears away this time.

"No secrets. Remember? Whatever it is...tell me. You'll feel better if you let it out."

"I wasn't trying to keep a secret. I just...I was thinking of myself and there is no reason to be thinking of myself at a time like this. But I can't stop crying. I keep trying to stop and I can't." Her voice cracked.

"And why, my beautiful wife, can't you stop crying?" I tried to massage her shoulders, but she felt stiff and uncertain. Usually my touch could calm her. But if anything she seemed more agitated.

"I wanted more children, James. I don't know how to accept the fact that I can't have any more. This wasn't the plan." She dropped her shoulders, letting my hand fall from her. "I wanted to fill our house with laughter and love..."

"Penny, it's okay. Plans change. And I love our family just the way it is. We have everything we need. The four of us is all I need." I tried not to think about how easily we could become three.

"You don't have to lie."

"I'm not lying." I tried to catch her gaze but she was looking anywhere but at me.

"You're acting like it doesn't matter. Like you don't remember what you said."

I shook my head, trying to think of what she was talking about. I grabbed her hands so she'd stop wiping her face, trying and failing to hide the fact that she was crying. "Remember what?"

She looked up at me with her tear stained eyes. "You said if it was up to you I'd be pregnant all the time. You can't stand there and pretend you're okay with this. I know you want more children. And I can't give you that. I can't give you the one thing you've asked of me."

How did she have this so wrong? How could she think that was all that I wanted, when all I truly wanted or needed was her. "Penny, all I've ever cared about is you." I knelt down in front of her so that she'd meet my eyes. "And then Scarlett came along and changed everything. Unexpectedly, I'd like to add. I would have been happy just the two of us. But I love her to pieces. And now Liam. Our children mean the world to me now. But I was always terrified when you were pregnant. I was always scared that something would go wrong. And it did. Yes, I wanted more children before this happened. But now? I don't know if I'd ever want you to get pregnant again even if we could. For weeks it felt like I'd lost you. I'll never jeopardize your health again. Another kid isn't worth the risk of losing you. I can't lose you."

She nodded but didn't stop crying. "I've always just wanted to give you everything you've wanted. Because I didn't come with…wealth or an Ivy League degree or a…"

I silenced her words with a kiss. "I never wanted those things. I only ever wanted you."

She wrapped one of her hands behind my neck and deepened the kiss. If I wasn't already on my knees, she would have brought me to them. Her kiss was salty from her tears. Her fingertips dug into the back of my neck, drawing me closer. When she was upset, there were usually two things that made Penny smile again. The first option was listening to her. Letting her get everything off her chest. The second option was distracting her. But this felt a lot more like she was trying to distract me. Which meant something else completely. She was still hiding something from me. Something that she thought after-sex bliss would make it easier for me to hear. I pulled back from her kiss, almost knocking both of us to the floor.

Her chest rose and fell rapidly as her eyes searched mine. "I wasn't done kissing you yet."

I just stared at her, waiting for her confession.

"What?" She pressed her lips together as she looked at me. A tell that meant I was absolutely right.

"I'm waiting to hear what else is on your mind."

"I'm pretty sure I made it pretty clear what was on my mind." Her eyes trailed down the front of my body.

"I meant besides that. You remember fragments. I remember everything, baby."

Her throat made an adorable squeaking noise. "You're acting like I did something bad."

"I didn't say you did anything bad. I'm saying you did something without asking me first."

"Well...yeah...I did that."

I raised my eyebrow.

Her eyes darted to my eyebrow and her throat made the same noise. "Sorry," she said and lightly touched the top of her chest. "I think I'm parched."

"Mhm. Out with it."

She sat back in her chair and grabbed a notebook from the desk. "Fine, you win. I talked to Porter and our lawyer and everyone thinks that Dr. Nelson will be staying in prison for the foreseeable future. But we will have to most likely provide testimony if it goes to trial. Which...I'm definitely nervous about. But if they hear directly from one of us it's more likely to stick. Not the correct legalese, but you get the idea."

"It's okay. I can handle that."

"Oh. Good." But she didn't look that relieved as she looked back down at the notebook. "We also have a flight to catch in a few hours. So we should probably pack."

I was not expecting that. At all. Hadn't she done enough running? Just when I thought I had her back, she completely reverted to her 19-year-old self again. "Penny, we can't go anywhere. Liam needs us here. He needs you."

"I know. That's why he's coming with us. We'll be flying with him. So we need to go pack." She looked back down at her notebook and flipped a page, her eyes scanning her notes.

"Penny, we can't just up and leave. Liam needs to be in the hospital. He needs the oxygen tubes and the machine that helps him breathe. He needs to be in a sterile environment."

"Right, he needs to be in *a* hospital. Not necessarily that one. James, the answer was right in front of us the whole time. Remember that huge donation you gave The University of New Castle after we left? I remember, because I didn't think you should have done it. The way they treated us left a sour taste in my mouth, but you did it anyway because you saw the good. It's where we met. It's where we fell in love. It was the start of our story."

"I remember."

"Well, they used that money to expand their curriculum. It helped them improve their medical program. And the best doctor that deals with preemies every day works there. He's our answer. He can fix Liam. And the best cardiologist in the country was luckily on vacation in Malibu this week. It was easy to get him to change his plans. He's meeting us there."

"I thought you liked your cardiologist?"

"I trust a doctor in New York as much as I trust those homeless people who pee on the subway."

"I don't think…"

"And he's not coming for me. I mean, I'll have him check out my heart murmur if you'd like. But he's coming for you."

I took a deep breath. "The doctors here have been looking after Liam just fine this whole time. I'm used to them. He's used to them. We're not moving him on a whim. And I'm fine. I've told you that I'm fine. All of this is completely unnecessary."

"You're not fine, James. You don't think I've seen you stop to catch your breath? You don't think I've seen you wince when you lift something? You're anything but fine."

"Penny…"

"And it's not a whim! I've spent all morning doing research and making calls." She flipped to another page in her notebook. "Eighty percent of Dr. Hughes' patients live past infancy. And…" she looked back down and pointed. "Thirty-seven percent of those patients go on to live normal, healthy lives. I know that number is still low, but…"

"We're supposed to talk to Liam's doctor this morning. Let's see what he has to say before we…"

"I've already talked to him. His numbers aren't this high. Not nearly this high."

"Penny…"

"And it's not just his projections. His hopes aren't this high. That's what matters here, James. He doesn't believe. But Dr. Hughes does. I told him all about our case. He believes in Liam. He thinks he can make our baby better."

"When you throw money at someone they'll tell you whatever you want to hear!" I regretted the words as soon as they left my mouth. She blinked back tears. She was trying. She was caring. That's all I had wanted from her in weeks. But moving Liam wasn't the answer. This wasn't what he needed. And what happened to being a team? We should have been making these decisions together. Before I told her what I thought, she started talking again.

"All of its already arranged. Everything's already booked. Ian's already agreed to come with us. I have to do this."

"You barely know anything about Liam's condition. You're still healing yourself. I think we should stay here."

"Then you can stay here." She pulled her notebook to her chest as she stood. "Liam and I are going to Newark. If you'll excuse me, I need to go pack."

"Penny…" I reached out for her, but she dodged my touch. "You promised you wouldn't leave me again." My defense was weak. I knew that. But I wasn't going to have her storm off angry with me. We had time to talk this through.

"I'm not leaving, James. I'm trying to save our son." The emotion was gone from her voice. She sounded tired. And defeated.

"Then have a conversation with me for five minutes instead of shoving statistics down my throat. I've been dealing with this problem myself for the past few weeks. I'm used to making the decisions here."

"Don't throw that in my face. You think I'm not upset that I wasn't there for him? It kills me. Why the hell do you think I'm doing this?"

I tried to take a slow breath. "If seeing Dr. Hughes is so important, we'll fly him here. I don't think Liam should be flying in a helicopter."

She wiped beneath her eyes. "He can't come here. I tried that."

"Then we'll find someone else."

"But he's the best. I've never cared about your money. I've never wanted fancy things. But in this one case I want to use it. This is all I'll ever ask for. I want to save our son."

"I do too. Of course that's what I want. I just don't know if this doctor is claiming the impossible. I've had other doctors come in to look at Liam. None of them have leapt to Dr. Hughes' conclusions. I haven't just been sitting here doing nothing. I've been doing my best."

"I didn't..." her voice trailed off. "That's not what I meant, James. I know you've done everything you could." She closed the distance between us. "I'm sorry."

"Me too." I grabbed one of her hands and squeezed it in mine. "I know that you wanted to be there for him. I didn't mean to suggest otherwise."

She nodded and locked eyes with me. "You know, I remember making a bet with you," she said.

I raised my eyebrow. I knew exactly where this was going. She had won the fucking thing. And now she was cashing in. "I remember. You won."

"Yeah, I won." Her voice was shaky. "We had a baby boy."

I tried to smile, but it felt like more of a grimace. I thought it was a girl. I really thought we'd have another girl. "You knew it all along."

She nodded. "And I get whatever I want? In the whole world?"

"That was the deal."

"I want Liam to live, James." Her voice cracked. "I want to do whatever it takes for him to be okay."

Her words broke my heart. "I don't know how to give you that. It's the one thing in the world I don't know how to give you."

She lifted up her notebook. "Dr. Hughes is a specialist that deals with the mental development of preemies. I'm telling you what I want here. I know what Liam needs. It doesn't matter that I was unconscious for the first two weeks of his life. He grew in my belly for months. I know him. And Dr. Hughes can fix him."

"Baby, we don't know if he'll live long enough for us to worry about his development."

"Yes we do." A tear fell down her cheek.

"We don't." I felt tears threatening to spill from my own eyes. I had heard all the numbers. I had done this same research. And I had done everything in my power to hold my family together. But I wasn't strong enough. I needed her. She was the glue that held this family together. She was the strength I lacked. And maybe she did know the answers that I didn't. Maybe she had found someone that could help Liam.

"Yes we do, James. He's going to live." There wasn't a doubt in her voice.

I wanted to believe her. I desperately wanted her to be right. "You don't know…"

"He kicked, James. We had a discussion and he kicked and that means he's going to stay and fight."

All throughout her pregnancy, Penny always claimed that Liam's constant kicking was him agreeing with her. That they were on the same page. I wasn't going to deny her this. And I wasn't going to risk my son's health because of my stubbornness. "Okay."

"Okay? And you'll come with us?"

"A bet is a bet."

"Thank you, James." She pressed her face to the side of my chest as she wrapped her arms behind my back. "I'm going to fix everything I broke."

And that's when I realized that she blamed everything that happened on herself. She was carrying the weight of the world on her shoulders. And I was letting her take it. Because I was tired. And she was right. I wasn't fine. But I didn't know how to tell her that. I didn't know how to tell her that I was having a hard time catching my breath. That my physical therapy wasn't helping. That I might need to have another surgery soon. We were already worried about our family becoming three instead of four. I didn't have the strength to tell her that it might become two instead.

PART 3

CHAPTER 13

Tuesday - *Penny*

Scarlett clung to me even tighter as Susan approached us.

"Hi, darling," Susan said. She put her hands on her knees and leaned down slightly. She looked stiff and uncertain and definitely didn't seem to know how to interact with children. And then she put out her hand. Like she was waiting for Scarlett to take it and kiss the back of it.

I tried to ignore Susan's oddities. I was on my knees with my arms wrapped around Scarlett, who refused to let go of me. "This is your grandma," I whispered in Scarlett's ear. "There's no reason to be afraid."

"I already have a grandma." She looked up at me with her eyes full of questions.

"Yeah. But you know how you have two grandpas? My dad and Daddy's dad?"

"Yes. I have two grandpas and only one grandma."

"Well, that's the thing, Scar. You have two grandmas too. This is Daddy's mother."

"No." She got really close to my ear and whispered, "It's the bad Dalmatian lady."

I stifled a laugh. Honestly Susan didn't look anything like Cruella de Vil. She didn't have half black hair and half white. She wasn't wearing any fur. I think it was probably more the air that Susan gave off. One of snobby sophistication. And maybe a slight tinge of murderiness. It was hard for me to like her too. But I was trying. For James' sake, we both had to try.

"Is she shy?" Susan asked. "That's a rather unfavorable characteristic. Come here child. I want to meet you."

"Actually Scarlett isn't shy at all. Are you, Scar?" I had been terribly shy growing up. I still was around new people. But my closest friends knew that I was quite talkative around anyone I was comfortable with. I tried to ignore Susan's snub. This wasn't about me. This was about our family being put back together. And this was part of that.

"I don't know what shy is," she whispered into my ear.

My sweet baby girl. I hugged her tightly and kissed the side of her forehead. "It's okay, go say hi to your other grandma." I reluctantly let go of her.

Susan put her hand back out for a friendly shake of some sort.

But Scarlett ducked under it and hugged her leg.

For a moment Susan looked like she didn't know what to do. And I watched in horror as she lifted her hand like she was going to pat my child on the head. Like a dog. But at the last minute she got down onto her knees, in her expensive dress and nylons and hugged my daughter back.

"Nice to meet you, Grandma," Scarlett said. "Do you want to see my room? I have lots of stuffies to play with."

"Stuffies?"

"Pandas and monkeys and all the zoo animals."

Susan looked up at me for help.

"Stuffed animals," I mouthed silently at her.

"Right. Stuffies. I'd love to see your collection," Susan said.

"Okay." Scarlett slipped her hand into Susan's and pulled her to the stairs.

"And you'll be good for your grandma, Uncle Rob, Aunt Daphne, Aunt Melissa, Uncle Josh, and Ellen?" I called after Scarlett.

"Yes." She said it as more of a question than a statement.

I didn't feel comfortable leaving her with just James' mother. Not yet. Maybe one day in the future, but that day wasn't today. James had insisted that Scarlett stay here in the city. Something about our apartment in Newark not being suitable for children. He did have a point. It was more of a sexy bachelor pad than a nice family home. Tons of sharp corners. Nothing was toddler-proof in the slightest.

So we had brought in reinforcements. Ellen was already here, which was a relief because Scarlett already viewed her as a grandmother. Rob, Daphne, and Sophie were on their way here to help. Melissa and Josh were exhausted from taking care of her last night. And I was pretty sure Melissa was still scrubbing the makeup off her face that Scarlett had applied. Besides, Rob wanted to introduce Daphne to her mother-in-law anyway. And Sophie to her new grandma. They could have a little reunion while we were away.

"You all set?" James asked.

"Mhm. Are you sure you don't want to bring her with us though?"

"It'll be good for her to get acquainted with my mother. Besides, we need some alone time. I have a lot to catch you up on."

I looked up at him. He basically just said, "We need to talk." I was about to ask him what he meant, but Scarlett rushed back into the room.

"Bye, Daddy." She flung herself into his arms.

He peppered her face with kisses, sending her into a fit of giggles. When he set her down she looked up at me.

"Bye, Mommy." She squinted her eyes at me. "Promise you'll come back?"

I knelt down and hugged her. "I promise, Scar."

"And you promise to bring Liam home? I've been waiting for him to see his room."

"I promise." I squeezed her tightly. *I promise, baby girl.*

***

"Let's head back to our place," James said. "Dr. Hughes needs some time to go over the lab results. He won't know anything until morning."

All day long I had been in a fit of nerves. First the helicopter ride. I had ended up getting engrossed enough in the story I had written to make the trip go faster. I read the whole thing, up to the words The End. Pieces that were missing had fallen back into place. And I was very aware of the fact that we were going back to the place where we first started. It felt like I'd be seeing it again with new eyes. Maybe more would come back to me. I desperately hoped I'd feel different than I did last time I was in Newark. I had driven there to escape from James. It felt more like I was going home now.

I'd also been nervous about waiting to meet Dr. Hughes. Then watching him poke and prod my son. And the talk that James wanted to have had never left the back of my mind.

I looked down at Liam in my arms. I didn't want to let him go. I didn't want to go back to the apartment with James and hear whatever he had to say. Because it was bad. I knew it was bad or he would have just told me here.

"The cardiologist is arriving in the morning as well," James said. "Let's go get some rest."

He lifted Liam out of my arms without me waiting to respond. He leaned down and whispered something in his ear. Liam squirmed in his grip and it almost looked like he smiled. James gently kissed his forehead.

I watched the scene with a smile of my own on my face. I was sorry that I wasn't there for Liam for the first few weeks of his life. But James had it covered. He had showered him with love. Liam hadn't been alone. I watched James gently place Liam into his incubator. The nurse attached all the tubes back to him and gave us a wave goodnight.

"I think he handled the transport pretty well, right? He doesn't seem to be any worse. I know you were worried that it wouldn't be good for him."

"He's strong. I was more worried about getting your hopes up." James pulled me into his side as we walked out of the NICU. "But this was a good idea. My hopes are up too. It's been a while since I've felt this hopeful, actually."

"That's good." I looked up at him as we exited the hospital. It seemed like he was telling the truth. He looked happy and relaxed. So what did we need to talk about?

The hot summer day had turned into a cool night. I closed my eyes for a moment, remembering it feeling just like this the night of that party so long ago. The night that James walked me home. I opened my eyes and stared out at Main Street. Some of the shops were different. Actually, a lot of them were. But our coffee shop still stood there, exactly the same. James had made sure of that.

I pulled him toward it. "I remember that day so perfectly. When we first met." I laughed, remembering James trying to reenact the scene to jog my memory. "I remember, James. And not just because I read about it. I really remember. Honestly, I think I remember everything except that last day. And that's probably for the best, right? So I'm all better." I wanted to throw my hands in the air to celebrate, but James was staring at me strangely.

He smiled down at me. But there was something sad in his smile. It didn't quite reach his eyes.

"James, what's wrong? Dr. Hughes sounded optimistic, didn't he? I know we have to wait for the test results, but…I think it's going to be good news."

"Nothing's wrong." He tucked a loose strand of hair behind my ear.

Lies. Why was he lying? "You said you had something to tell me. What is it?"

"Let's head back to the apartment. I think we could both use a drink."

In all the years I had been with him, he never said he needed a drink. He certainly never suggested that I needed one. It felt like my stomach turned over. Something was wrong. He was hiding something big from me. And I wasn't going to wait another second to hear whatever it was. I pulled away from him. "James. Just tell me. You said it yourself, your hopes are up. Everything is looking good. We should be enjoying this moment instead of…" I gestured at him. "Whatever it is you're doing right now."

His sigh was heavy. "I didn't tell you everything when you woke up. You didn't remember me. You didn't remember our family. I didn't want to add any stress to that equation. But you're good now. And Liam…Liam…"

My heart ached. "I talked to Liam's doctor back in New York. I know about all the issues. And the potential ones down the line. He told me everything. He answered all my questions."

"It's not about Liam. I'm sorry. I was just…trying to find the right words." He looked nervous and upset.

The sinking feeling in the pit of my stomach grew. A sinking feeling that felt so familiar. A pain that felt like it was happening in that moment. I cringed.

"Penny, are you okay?" His voice sounded far away. "Let's just get you back to the apartment." He put his hand on my lower back to guide me where he wanted.

"No." I pushed him off. "The man I married didn't rely on substances for the strength to tell me the truth. Whatever it is, just tell me. Tell me, James!"

"I'm not trying to get you drunk. Jesus." He ran his fingers through his hair. "I just feel like we should both at least be sitting down. I need to sit down."

My stomach flipped over again. And everything came back in a flash.

I opened the door and smiled down at my daughter.

"Hi, Mommy." She looked up at me in a strange way. As if she were studying me.

"Hi, Scar, I missed you." I bent down to hug her but she ran past me.

"Ellie!" she screamed.

I tried not to show the disappointment on my face. I had told myself that she wanted to hang out with Rob because she missed her father and wanted to hang out with another male in James' absence. But that wasn't the case. She seemed perfectly content as Ellen picked her up.

"Hi, sweet girl," Ellen said. "Did you have fun at the office?"

"Yes! I got to play with the copy machine."

I glanced at Rob.

He shrugged his shoulders.

"Come in," I said. "I hope she wasn't a nuisance."

"Nah, it was fun. Soph never wants to come to work with me. Everyone doted on her all morning. They couldn't stop talking about her beautiful red hair."

"Mhm." I looked over at Scar. Ellen was taking her upstairs to play. Ellen could entertain her for hours, yet she didn't want to spend one minute alone with me.

"James called last night to say goodnight to Scarlett. And he may have mentioned that you needed this."

I smiled and grabbed the grocery bag that I hadn't noticed. "I love you so much, Rob." I pulled out the pint of Ben and Jerry's Chunky Monkey ice cream. "Do you want some?"

"I've never turned down ice cream before."

We walked into the kitchen and I grabbed two spoons. "Did you already have lunch? I'm sure we have something more substantial to go with this."

"We grabbed hot dogs on the way here. Scarlett insisted."

"Of course she did." We made our way into the family room. I took the top off the ice cream container as I sat down on the couch, and then I took a huge bite. "God, it's everything I've been craving and more."

Rob laughed as he took a bite. "It's good, but it's not orgasmic, Penny."

I shook my head and laughed. "It's all I've been craving since the wedding." I put my hand on the center of my chest.

"Hey, are you okay?"

"I'm fine." I immediately removed my hand and took another bite. "I just have indigestion or something." I frowned at my own words. I had barely eaten anything in the past two days. What would I be having indigestion from? "Being pregnant sucks."

Rob laughed. "Daphne's getting into that phase too. Pregnant women. Ugh."

I lightly shoved his shoulder and tried not to wince at the pain that had now shifted to my stomach.

"Seriously, are you okay? You look really pale."

"Nothing a little ice cream can't fix." I took another bite and forced myself to swallow. Now I felt incredibly nauseous. "So what deal was James trying to land?"

Rob laughed. "How should I know?"

I set the pint of ice cream down on the coffee table. "Rob, you're the CEO. Shouldn't you know everything that's going on?" I smiled at him.

"Yeah, and I do." He said it a little defensively.

"Okay, so what deal is James trying to get for Hunter Tech in London?"

"I have no idea what you're talking about." Another pain shot through my stomach and I leaned forward slightly. "You asked him to go to London."

"What? No, I didn't. He's not there for Hunter Tech."

Ow. "What do you mean? Why else would he go to London?"

"I don't know. I thought it was for the university."

"He's not teaching an abroad program." I laughed awkwardly. "Seriously, Rob, why was he in London?"

"I don't know. But the paparazzi probably do." He picked up his phone and typed something in. He lowered both his eyebrows.

"What?" I asked.

"Nothing." He tried to move his phone away from me but I grabbed it.

He had done a Google image search. There were tons of images of James dining with some woman at an outdoor restaurant. Some gorgeous woman with long, brunette hair and skin that was too tan for London's dreary climate. "Who is this woman?" I asked.

"I don't know, I've never seen her before."

I laughed. "Is this some kind of weird joke, Rob? One of your pranks?" I stared at him hopefully and tried to ignore the pain in my chest. What the fuck was James doing with some beautiful woman in London? And why had he lied to me about it?

"I'm sure there's an innocent explanation," Rob said. "He should be back pretty soon, right?"

I glanced at the clock. "In about an hour."

"I should probably get back to work." Rob abruptly stood up.

"Rob."

He seemed to cringe.

"Is he cheating on me?"

Rob laughed. "No, of course not. He wouldn't." But there was doubt in his voice. Suspicion. And maybe, just maybe, a small hint of anger. I just didn't know if it was directed at me or his brother.

"Rob? If you know something you have to tell me." I stood up and immediately hunched forward.

"Penny?"

I felt his hands on my shoulders. "Ow." I put my hand on my stomach. I didn't realize I had said it out loud. But by the look on Rob's face, I definitely had.

"Penny, are you alright?"

"No." I shook my head. "I'm going to be sick."

"Okay...just..." his voice trailed off as he ran into the kitchen.

Fuck. I grabbed my stomach.

Rob came back just in time with a bowl.

I sat down on the carpet and threw up. Every little bit that was left in my stomach barely covered the bottom of the bowl.

He ran his hand up and down my back. "Do you want me to get Ellen?"

I shook my head. "No. I don't want Scar to see me like this." I leaned over the bowl again. My stomach still ached, but nothing else seemed to want to come up.

Rob handed me a paper towel.

"I'm so sorry." I wiped my mouth off.

"I'm the one that should be apologizing. The ice cream I brought made you sick."

"No, it's probably just really late morning sickness. I'm fine." Fuck, it hurts.

"I think I should take you to the doctor."

I shook my head. "Rob," I said and looked up at him. "Is James having an affair? Tell me he's not. Please." It felt like my heart was ripping in two. Something was wrong. Something was terribly wrong.

"No." He said it firmly this time. The doubt was gone. And then I felt it. A wetness surrounding me. It was too soon. Panic started to weigh on top of the searing pain in my stomach. "My water broke," I croaked. Two months too early. I felt tears welling in my eyes.

"Shit," Rob said. "I'll get Ellen."

"No. Scar can't see me like this." I grabbed his leg. "Help me up. William will take me to the hospital."

"Penny..."

"Please, Rob. Scar already thinks I'm weak. She can't see me like this." I tried to blink away the tears. "I don't want her to see me like this." I leaned over in pain.

Rob pulled out his cell phone. "My sister-in-law's water just broke," he said into the cell phone. "Twenty minutes, are you fucking kidding me?" He hung up the phone. "Okay, I'm going to help you up." He leaned down and grabbed my hands.

I grimaced in pain. "Something's wrong. It's too soon." It didn't feel the way it had when my water broke when I was pregnant with Scarlett. Everything felt wrong.

"It's okay," Rob said as he slowly helped me to my feet. But then something in his face changed. Horror. Dread. Agony. They swept over his features in a flash.

I suddenly felt faint and I teetered forward slightly.

"Ellen!" he yelled at the top of his lungs. *"Ellen, call William and tell him to get the car started!"*

I winced in pain. Why was he calling for her? I had just asked him not to.

Ellen came running down the stairs and gasped. The look of horror on her face matched Rob's.

I followed her trail of vision and stared down at the pool of blood at my feet. Seeping into the carpet. Dripping down my legs. The blood was everywhere.

"You're okay," Rob said as he scooped me up into his arms and started running. *"You're going to be okay."*

But I wasn't. I just knew I wasn't. Because the pain in my stomach was growing worse by the second. And my son wasn't kicking me. He wasn't fucking kicking me.

"Christ!" Rob yelled as he slammed his fist against the elevator button.

Porter and Briggs ran out of their office down the hall.

"What happened?" Porter asked. He reached out to take me from Rob.

I grabbed the collar of Rob's shirt. I didn't want him to let me go.

"I've got her," Rob said.

"This way then," Porter said and ran toward the staircase.

"I'll call James," Briggs said and ran back to their office.

I closed my eyes. Each step downwards on the stairs made my stomach ache more. I heard a car door open and close.

I heard the squeal of the tires. Cursing. I had never felt more weak. It felt like the life was draining out of my body. And not just my son's. My own. My heartbeat seemed to slow. A chill entered my bloodstream. It felt like the coolness was pulsing through my whole body.

"It's okay," Rob said. *"We're almost there."* I was vaguely aware of the fact that he hadn't set me down in the back seat. That he was cradling me in his arms. Like he knew if he let go, I'd be gone.

"Take care of him," I said.

"Penny." His hand on my cheek felt scalding hot.

"Promise me you'll take care of him."

"You're going to be alright. Everything's okay."

I looked up at his face. It was wet with tears. I had seen him cry once before. When James had gotten shot. When we thought we might lose him. And I knew it then. He thought I was going to die. I thought I was going to die. And I felt the death in my stomach. I felt it rip my heart in two.

"Promise me." My voice came out as a whisper.

He shook his head.

"Take care of Scarlett."

"Penny..."

"Take care of my family."

"We're almost there," he said.

"I'm scared." I tried to grab his hand, but my grip was too weak. The pain was easing as the feeling of ice spread. It was peaceful. Like my body was trying to comfort me as I slipped. As it became harder to breathe. "I'm so scared," I whispered.

"Penny, open your eyes."

I tried, but I couldn't.

"Penny, you're not allowed to leave us. Do you hear me? Open your eyes, okay?"

But I couldn't. I couldn't do it.

"Please."

The desperation in his voice pained me. But I couldn't frown. I couldn't move at all.

"Fucking open your eyes!"

The memory disappeared as quickly as it had come. I took a deep breath and tried to swallow down the agony. This whole time James had been saying it was better if I hadn't remembered that day. And that was why. He hadn't been there when I needed him. He'd been with someone else.

James was looking at me with concern etched on his face. I stared into the depths of his dark brown eyes. Once I thought that they swirled with secrets. But now? It was love in his eyes. It had been for so long. I stared at the small crinkles by his eyes that I loved so much. The stubble on his jaw. His lips that kissed me goodnight. That told me I was his one and only. That I willingly believed.

"Is everything okay?" he asked.

No. I swallowed hard. *You cheated on me. How could you cheat on me?* That's what he wanted to talk about. It had to be. That's why he looked guilty. He was right, I would need a drink to hear the specifics. Because I didn't understand why he'd do it. But I also knew that I didn't want to hear about it at all. If he did it and it was over…I could live with that, right? I could forgive him. I searched his face. "Whatever it is you want to talk about…can it wait? Until after Liam is better? I can't do this right now. Or maybe not at all." I bit the inside of my lip. "Not at all. Definitely. I don't want to know."

"Penny, it's important. I should have told you sooner, but I was worried…"

"It's okay. It's okay." I hugged him, pressing the side of my face against his chest. I listened to his steady heartbeat. *It's going to be okay.* My life without him would be meaningless and without purpose. I needed him. I'd take whatever part of him he'd offer. And besides, he came back to me. He fought so hard to win me over the past few weeks. He was there with me every moment. *Except for when you went into labor and he was with another woman. When you really needed him and only his brother was there. Stop.*

It didn't matter. He wouldn't have tried to help me remember if he wasn't sorry. He could have left. He could have never come back. But he was here. Right here. Holding me. I squeezed him tighter and then pulled away. "Are you hungry? I'm hungry. We should get pizza. And I think I will take that drink."

His Adam's apple rose and then fell. "Okay. Grottos sounds perfect to me too." He tucked me into his side and guided us toward my favorite pizza joint.

I wanted to be happy that my memories were all intact. That we were here to help Liam. That for just one moment, everything had been so normal. I never even realized how much I craved normalcy until a minute ago. But all I could focus on now was the thought of James' infidelities. Was it just that once? More?

All I knew for sure was that he didn't want me to remember the day that I had Liam. That it would be for the best. So why was he going to bring it up now? I could keep pretending like I didn't remember. I'd pretend my whole life if it meant he still wanted me. I kept trying to push the memory aside. To let it go. To stomp on it and set it on fire and burn it to hell. But it just sat there. Right at the forefront of my thoughts. *Stop.*

A hostess guided us to our table. She was probably a college student, still here for the summer. Most likely as young as I had been when I met James. I stared daggers at her.

"Thanks," James said as she showed us to our seats. He smiled at her before she walked away.

Was James checking her out? It seemed like he was checking her out. Who smiles at a stranger so sincerely? Would he sneak out of our apartment tonight and come back to her? It felt like I had a knife in my heart. Slowly twisting. Was this how it would always be now? Me wondering what if?

"Penny, I really need to get this off my chest." He reached across the table and lowered the menu from my hands.

"To make you feel better? Or is this for me?" I wasn't sure where the question came from. But it was true. This wasn't about me. He'd feel better if he admitted it. I wouldn't. I'd feel like fucking shit.

He opened his mouth and then closed it again. "Both."

I stared at him. If that was true, maybe I was wrong about what this was about. What if where he was the day I went into labor was a misunderstanding? I stared into his eyes. "You're sure about that?"

He shook his head and it looked like he was gazing behind me, lost in thought. "It would make me feel better. I don't like keeping things from you."

That already felt like a confession to me. "Is whatever you have to say going to hurt me?"

He looked pained. "I'm sorry, Penny."

The waiter walked over and asked if we were ready to order. James immediately sent him away before I could even open my mouth.

I stared at my husband. It didn't seem like he was going to let this go. The confession was tearing him apart. He looked more tired than ever. He looked the way I felt. Defeated. Truly and utterly defeated.

"James, if getting this secret off your chest is only going to benefit you, I don't want to hear it," I said.

"But you need to know."

"I don't want to know. Can't you talk to your therapist about this instead of me? Get it off your chest with him? And we can just keep...living. We can pretend everything is normal until it becomes normal again."

The pain in his eyes seemed to sharpen as he stared at me. The vulnerability was gone. Now he just looked pissed at me. "I want to talk to my wife. Not a stranger."

"Dr. Green is hardly a stranger. You've been seeing him for longer than I've known you. He can help you work through this, right?"

"I haven't been seeing him for the past few weeks."

"Why?"

"Because there's no point." Everything that came out of my mouth just made him angrier. "Penny, you can't just hide from the truth no matter how much it hurts. This isn't just about me. It's about you too."

"Really? It's about me? So it's my fault?" *Asshole.*

"What? That's not…"

"God, James. All I've ever done was love you."

"I know. And all I've ever done was love you." He reached for my hands across the table, but I pulled mine onto my lap.

"You have a funny way of showing it."

He sighed, like talking to me was the most exhausting thing he ever had to do. "Penny, I know this is going to be hard to hear. But we need to make the proper plans just in case. For the sake of the children. For your sake too."

"For my sake?" I realized I had raised my voice and that people were starting to stare. I leaned forward and hissed, "Are you fucking kidding me? My sake, James? If you had been thinking about me at all you never would have let any of this happen."

He stared at me. "I've done the best that I could. But my heart hasn't been the same since our wedding day. You know that. I know we've never talked about it, but you knew that. You had to have known that."

I'm pretty sure my mouth was hanging open. It reminded me of something Isabella had said to me once. That he was only interested in the chase. That once he got my heart, he'd get bored and move on to the next thing. The next rush of adrenaline. The next fix. "You don't love me anymore." I didn't ask it like a question. If what he was saying was true, it was a fact. James' heart didn't belong to me anymore. He'd been slipping away ever since our wedding day.

"What? No, that's not…"

"Just stop. I know, okay? I know. And…I don't want to know any more. I saw the picture. Her face is already burned in my brain. So whatever specifics you have, keep them to yourself."

"Who are you talking about? What picture?"

"That tan brunette woman you were with in London. You weren't with me when I went into labor. I was so scared and you weren't there. But you more than made it up to me the past few weeks. So I forgive you. Let's just move past this." I was grasping at straws. He had made it pretty clear that we were done. But I couldn't accept that. I just couldn't. I picked up the menu and stared at it even though I already knew the whole thing by heart. And all I ever ordered was cheese pizza. Boring. No wonder he didn't love me anymore. I wasn't exciting or alluring or anything. I was just…me.

"You remembered? When did you remember that?"

"Outside. Right before we came in here. So you don't have to fill in the details. You cheated on me. But you're here now. That's all that matters." If that was true, why had I started crying? Why did it feel like he was slipping away from me before he even utter the words divorced?

"I wasn't in London cheating on you."

A strangled laugh escaped my lips. "There's no point in lying to me now. Isn't that what you've been trying to get off your chest? You made me pull it from you. And now here we are. What am I supposed to do with that?" *What the fuck am I going to do with the rest of my life?* I was moments away from bursting into tears or holding a knife to our innocent hostess' throat if he glanced over my shoulder one more freaking time.

"I'd never cheat on you."

"I remembered everything, James. Why are you backpedaling now? And I was wrong, I do need to know. What was it exactly that made you do it? Was it something that I did? I feel like I've given you everything I possibly could." If I wasn't enough for him...no matter how much I didn't want him to go...how could I possibly ask him to stay?

"You have." That was all he said. Like it was enough. It still looked like his mind was far away. Like he didn't care about this conversation at all, even though it was slowly killing me.

"Then what were you doing in London?" I asked. "Why were the tabloids covered in pictures of the two of you? What could possibly whisk you away from me during the last trimester of my pregnancy? Especially when you claimed to be so worried about my health." What a joke. Our whole life together was a lie.

He shook his head. But didn't say anything at all.

"None of this even makes sense. Getting married shouldn't have changed how you felt about me. You wanted to be married. You proposed to me, not the other way around. If you didn't want me, why did you propose? Why?"

Nothing. He had nothing to say.

I shook my head. "It's my fault. I kept postponing our wedding. I wanted to move to New York City first and settle in. I wanted to finish school. I kept delaying it...making you love the chase even more."

I couldn't read his expression. Maybe he wasn't saying anything because he thought I had lost my mind. Or maybe he just cared that little. He had checked out of this conversation five minutes ago. He wasn't even humoring my questions with responses. He was just staring at me.

"And all those times you've been possessive and jealous? Was that just a show? I can't even count how many times you've been a jerk to Tyler for no reason at all. And no wonder. Because your idea of a marriage has blurred lines. So of course you assumed he was cheating on Hailey with me. Because that's what you would do. You son of a bitch." I grabbed a drink off a waiter's passing tray and threw the contents into James' face.

He looked surprised, but still said nothing as the liquid dropped from his stupid perfect eyelashes.

"Tell yourself whatever you have to in order to not turn to a new vice. Because despite what a prick you are, my heart never changed. I've always loved you, you stupid fucking ass-hat. Have fun with the brunette." I stormed out of the restaurant before I burst into tears.

CHAPTER 14

Tuesday - *James*

She thought I cheated on her. I watched the whole scene unfold like I wasn't even there. As soon as I realized what she thought I was going to discuss, I didn't even try to correct her. I let her believe it. My chest hurt. She was right. Not about the cheating, but about why I didn't want her to remember the day she went into labor. I wasn't there for her when she needed me. She was in pain and I wasn't even in the country.

But cheating on her? Not a chance in hell. Never. I couldn't even imagine being with another woman. Penny meant every-thing to me.

I watched her disappear out the front doors of the restaurant. And still I did nothing. I just sat there trying to think of the best way to approach this situation. I grabbed a napkin and wiped off my face. Luckily Penny had grabbed a glass of water instead of a sticky soda or cocktail.

People were staring at me. The whole restaurant had erupted in whispers. I could have run after her. I could have at least walked out and away from the rumors that were already spread-ing like wildfire.

But I couldn't move. All I could think about was that maybe this was for the best. My chest hurt all the time. Some nights I'd wake up clutching my chest like my heart was about to explode. I knew something wasn't right. My cardiologist had mentioned another surgery. He had mentioned the risks. That's what I wanted to talk to her about tonight. I had to tell her what was going on with me.

I looked down at the wet napkin clutched in my hand. Would it be easier for Penny this way though? If I died with her hating me? I didn't want to die alone. I pictured her by my bedside holding my hand. Not far away cursing the day I was ever born. I couldn't imagine her telling our children that I was a cheat. A liar. A bad husband and father. And I couldn't live another second without her by my side anyway. I cared more about her than life itself.

What the fuck am I doing? I stood up and threw the napkin down on the table. Penny needed to know the truth. No matter how much it hurt. No matter how much it pained both of us. I couldn't face this alone. And we needed more time. Time to enjoy our life together. Just more...time. I wasn't ready to run out of it.

I ran out of the restaurant and looked both ways on Main Street. Where had she gone? A drop of rain fell on the tip of my nose. I glanced up as the sky opened and it began to pour.

I looked down the street at my old apartment building. And then I ran in the opposite direction. I knew my wife, and that wasn't where she'd go. There was only one place I felt drawn to right now. I let my feet guide me. I was half of a whole. Penny thought that I meant my feelings had changed the day we got married when I was literally talking about the health of my heart. But my heart belonged to her. That's why I wasn't surprised when I saw a flash of red entering Smith Hall when I turned onto the green.

She had been stuck in the past for a few weeks. There were so many moments in our relationship that stuck out to me. But the point of no return? It happened in Smith Hall. I was soaked by the time I reached the front doors, and completely out of breath. I put my hands on my knees, gulping for air. The rain continued to fall harder, drawing steam up from the hot sidewalk.

I remembered that night I saw her walking alone on Main Street. She had been wearing this ridiculously short sparkly skirt and a white tank top. Freaking white in the rain. I didn't stand a chance. My thoughts had already been straying to her whenever I wasn't focused on planning assignments. But after that? She consumed me. Her shy smile. The way she so easily laughed about her own shortcomings. And the way the rain on her skin made her glisten. Like she was an angel sent here to save me.

And she had saved me. From myself. I was self-destructive and bitterly lonely. I owed her for the life she had given me the past several years. Even if that life got cut short, whatever amount of time I had with her was better than anything without her.

I pushed through the doors and made my way as quickly as I could up the stairs in the darkness. The only light in the building was coming from a room upstairs. A room I was all too familiar with. My wet shoes squished as I stopped in front of my old office. It belonged to someone else now. His belongings were all over the desk and there were certificates on the walls that were once bare. But it still felt the same. Like I was stepping back in time.

I wanted to smile at the memory of her balling up her grade in her fist and throwing it on the floor. Or of her poking me in the middle of the chest calling me out on my shit. Or taking her for the first time, right on top of that very desk.

But it was hard to smile when she was sitting at that same desk crying. Her face was pressed against her arm, her body heaving up and down as she let the grief take over her. I didn't want to see her grieving now. Not until she needed to be.

"Penny?"

She lifted her head up and looked at me. Her clothes were soaked and mascara was smudged under her eyes. She was a beautiful mess. My beautiful mess. And I wouldn't let her think otherwise for another second.

I stepped into the room and closed the door behind me. "You're everything to me. Every. Single. Thing."

"You cheated on me." Tears streamed down her cheeks.

"Never."

"You stopped loving me."

"Impossible."

"You don't want to be with me anymore."

"That couldn't be farther from the truth. I want to be with you every second of every day." *Until I take my dying breath.*

"Then why were you in London?" She shoved the chair back from the desk and stood up. Her sadness was replaced with anger. She looked like she wanted to punch me. "Who was that woman you were with? Why else would you not want me to remember that day?"

"Because I wasn't there when you needed me. And I'll feel guilty about that until the day I die." Most people said those words with empty promises. But my day was sooner than she realized. And I meant every word.

"And the brunette?"

"I wanted to give you a present before Liam was born. The book you wrote is brilliant. Those agents that rejected you wouldn't know a good piece of fiction if you shoved it down their throats. I got you what you wanted. And going with a London imprint provides more anonymity. I have all the papers back in New York. From what I can tell, the advance is very generous. They just need your signature."

The anger disappeared from her face. "She's a literary agent?" She shook her head and the anger was back.

"*Your* literary agent. If you want. Of course it's up to you. But I wanted to give your book the exposure it deserved."

She scoffed. "The kind I could never get based off of the words I wrote alone?"

"That's not…"

"You promised you wouldn't interfere. I wanted to do this one thing on my own."

"And you still can if you want to. Or you can take the deal. It's good, Penny. She was passionate about the project."

"Or was she passionate about getting to work with you?" She lifted up a stapler off the desk and threw it at me.

I dodged it and it slammed against the wall, exploding staples every which way. "What the hell was that?"

"We'll never know if I had what it takes now, James! I asked you not to help me!" She picked up a cup filled with pens.

I held up my hands in front of me. "I wanted to surprise you."

"By sneaking around behind my back and making me think you were being unfaithful?!" She threw the cup at me. "Spoiler alert, your fake affair didn't worsen the blow!"

I dodged the cup but got hit by a few stray pens. "Penny, I did it for you!"

"For me? Really? Because I had this one thing. One thing I did on my own. Can't you see how much I needed this? God!" She wiped underneath her eyes, spreading more blackness across her cheeks. "I need a few minutes alone." She turned away from me. "Just…get out."

"It's my office."

She stormed over to me. "Not anymore. And I'm not some naïve 19-year-old girl upset about a grade. This meant everything to me, James." She poked me in the middle of the chest. "It's the only thing I ever wanted to do on my own and you fucked it all up. You did the exact opposite of what I wanted. It's like you don't listen to me at all. I don't know why I ever let you read it in the first place."

It was like she had turned back time. She was a student again. Yelling at me about her grade. I felt my cock harden, pressing against the front of my pants. All I wanted to do was bend her over and spank her perfect ass. I loved how worked up she was. There was nothing better than fucking her when she was pissed off at me.

She made the first move before. All those years ago, her anger turned to passion. Today it didn't look like she was going to stop being angry anytime soon. So I made the first move before I busted the zipper on my pants.

I grabbed the back of her neck, pulling her lips to mine. I expected her to push me away. To slap me. To tell me to screw myself. Instead, she moaned into my mouth. I let my hands slip to her ass and lifted her legs around me. Her body fused with mine as I slammed her back against the adjacent wall. A certificate swung off its nail and crashed to the floor.

Penny tugged on my hair to deepen the kiss, but I pulled away.

"I'm sorry," I whispered against her lips, our breath colliding in pants.

Her fingers dug into the back of my neck. "I don't forgive you," she said. But her voice was airy with desire. She knew how similar this was to our first time. She wanted this just as badly as I did. Which was why the next few words came out so easily.

"You're infuriating, Penny."

"Then punish me, Professor Hunter."

God. Damn. We'd had sex once in three weeks. Once. I wasn't just a professor pining over the forbidden. This was my wife. I had already tasted her. I was already addicted to her touch. This wasn't about savoring a moment that had to be a one-time thing. It was about claiming what was mine. Because it didn't matter that she was pissed at me or that I was running out of time. This woman had my heart in the palm of her hand.

I didn't need to go slow. I wasn't interested in making love to her on my old desk. I needed to fuck her. I needed to show her that she belonged to me and only me.

I pulled her off the wall, ignoring the sound of something smashing against the floor. I shoved the contents of the desk to the ground and placed her on the edge of it, making quick work of her shorts as she reached for the zipper of my pants.

"I'd hate it when we fought if it didn't turn me on so much," she said as she wrapped her hand around my length.

Most days I was pretty sure I had dreamed her to life. There was no one more perfect for me than her. I was seconds away from confessing everything. From falling into a pit of despair I wasn't sure I could get out of.

I'd tell her later. After I had her one more time with her looking at me the way she was right now. Like I was her rock. Like I'd always be there for her.

CHAPTER 15

Tuesday - *Penny*

There was something in his eyes that I couldn't quite read. Guilt maybe? It was gone in an instant. Just like my anger was gone the moment he thrust inside of me.

Jesus. The first time we'd had sex, it was almost like he was trying to fuck me out of his system. Hard. Rough. Hot. I waited for the memory to slip away, just like all my other ones had come in a rush and slowly fell back in place where they belonged. But this one didn't go away. And I had the eeriest sensation that James was trying to get me out of his system again. That he'd pull away from me in a moment and claim this was just a one-time thing. Or a one-last-time thing in this case.

It was hard to focus on what felt off when he felt so amazing inside of me. But no matter how amazing this was, something wasn't right. "Is something wrong?" I panted. Instead of sounding concerned, my voice came out wanting.

He kissed the side of my neck, ignoring my question. And then lightly bit down on my earlobe.

I tilted my head to the side. I loved when he did that. He bit down harder as one of his hands slid down my stomach. His fingers stopped just above the spot that was desperately craving his attention. Almost like he was trying to distract me from my prying.

"James." It came out as a moan instead of an inquiry. I reached up to grab the sides of his face so that he'd look at me.

But he yanked my tank top down, trapping my arms against the sides of my torso as he started fucking me harder. I felt my ass digging into the edge of the desk with each thrust. It felt amazing but I wanted him to look me in the eyes. I lowered my shoulder to try and pull my arm out of my tank top.

He pulled harder, spilling my breasts from the cups of my bra and pinning my arms more firmly. I tried to lift my arm again. He wasn't looking at me. Why wasn't he looking at me?

My thoughts disappeared as his lips encircled one of my nipples. He tugged with his teeth. *Fuck.* I felt my hips arch up to meet his thrusts. He grabbed my hips, lifting my ass slightly off the desk and slammed into me even harder. Faster.

God. Loving him had always made me feel free. Free from concern. Free from right and wrong. Free from judgment. But I didn't feel that way tonight. I felt like I was paying for something. Like he was taking a piece of my soul and I had no idea what he was going to do with it.

Each thrust pulled me closer and closer to the edge. It would have been easy to get lost in the moment if I didn't know him so well. If I didn't know that something was truly wrong.

I squirmed beneath him until I was finally able to wiggle my arms out of my tank top and bra. I reached for his face again, but before I could, he grabbed my hands and slammed the backs of them against the desk. They hit something, sending the object to the ground with a loud crash.

The noise made me jolt. A groan escape from James' mouth.

"James, is the door locked? Someone might walk in."

He leaned over me, his stubble scratching my cheek. I wasn't sure why, but the sensation pushed me so close to the edge.

Maybe because the feeling of his scruff was usually accompanied by him whispering something dirty and delicious in my ear. Something about how much I loved the thrill of getting caught. Something that would make me spread my legs a little wider for him.

"I love you, Miss Taylor," he said instead.

Before I could respond, he pressed down on my clit, pushing me over the edge. "James!"

I felt the warmth of him inside of me. A feeling I'd never grow tired of. I tried to catch my breath. I was completely spent. For a moment, nothing else mattered. It didn't matter that we were technically in some random professor's office. Or that a piece of our hearts were in the nearby hospital. All that mattered was that we were together. I savored the feeling of how safe I felt in his arms.

And then I felt a wetness on the side of my neck.

"James?" I reached for the sides of his face and pulled up, but he kept his mouth against my skin, leaving a trail of kisses down the front of my chest. *Lower.* A tingle of desire swept through my stomach even though he had just pleased me. He was distracting me on purpose, but I felt immobile. He said he hadn't cheated on me. He'd told me about getting me a publishing deal. Everything was already off his chest. *Right?* I swallowed hard. *Right?*

He stopped at one of my scars and kissed it lightly. "I love you," he whispered against my skin.

I felt more wetness. Not the feeling of a kiss at all. It was...was he crying? "James?"

He kissed another of my scars. "I'm so sorry." His voice cracked.

I sat up, not caring that a random sheet of paper was stuck to my back. Or that I was sitting on someone's daily planner. Or that I was half naked in a room that someone could easily walk into. Nothing mattered but the man in front of me.

James fell to his knees and kissed the inside of my shin, keeping his eyes downcast.

I tried to stifle the fear gripping my heart. "It's okay," I said. "About the publishing deal. I don't know if I'm going to take it...but I know you did it out of love. I'm sorry that I overreacted."

He still didn't look up at me.

I pulled myself off the desk and knelt down beside him. "I'm not mad." I still would have been if he wasn't acting like this. But this moment made me realize just how arbitrary being upset really was. I never wanted to cause James to look the way he looked now. I never wanted to cause him pain. I'd forgive him a million times if it meant he'd look at me.

"James." I lifted his head toward mine. I felt his tears on my fingers even though he was still avoiding my gaze. "James, talk to me."

A strangled noise escaped his throat. His body heaved up and down. I had never seen him like this. He broke in front of me. The guard he always had up shattered. There was a vulnerability there that he had never let me see before.

I tried to wipe away his tears like he so often did for me. "James." I was pretty sure my voice sounded as broken as he looked. "Please look at me. Talk to me. What's wrong?" I felt like I was drowning. Screw cheating. Screw publishing deals. Screw every tiny little thing. Whatever had caused this reaction in James was so much bigger. So much worse.

He slowly lifted his face to mine. "No one ever talks about the consequences of loving someone," he said. "I didn't know about the consequences. I'm so sorry. I'm so sorry, baby."

Consequences? What was he talking about? "That's because there aren't any consequences…"

"Breaking someone?" He immediately shook his head. "Hurting someone? Those are consequences. It's easy to get caught up in your own emotions. But I never realized how much love could hurt the other person."

"Well those things don't happen in true love."

He just stared at me.

"They don't happen to *us*. Because no matter what struggles we face we have each other."

He shook his head.

For some reason I found myself mimicking his actions. "No? Is that what you're saying? No?"

He just kept shaking his head.

"Well, I don't accept that. I've seen a horrible reality in which we didn't become an us. I'm not going back to that. You fought so hard for me to remember. And I remember everything. Every little thing. All I know is that it's you and me against the world, James. Us together. Whatever it is that's upsetting you, it's actually inconsequential. I'm sure of it. I've never been so sure of anything in my entire life. It's you and me, James. It's you and me. Forever."

What I said made everything worse. He seemed to be gulping for air. "I'm sorry."

I shifted closer to him. "I think you're having a panic attack. I'm going to call the hospital. Where's your phone?" I stood up to look around, but he grabbed my hand.

He finally lifted his gaze to mine, locking me in place. He looked tormented. Another ragged breath escaped from his lips. I felt paralyzed as he opened his mouth.

"My surgery didn't work," he said.

I couldn't breathe.

"I'm in pain all the time."

It felt like my heart stopped beating.

"The physical therapy isn't helping."

His words were jumbling in my head.

"I need another surgery. But my body isn't strong enough right now."

The words stopped shifting around in my head. What was he trying to say?

"I've tried everything."

My breath came back in a rush. *No.* "Okay." I nodded. "So you'll have another surgery when you've had more time to recover. The cardiologist that's coming tomorrow will have another look at you. We'll figure this out. Just like we always do."

"It's not that simple."

"Yes it is. That's why we're here. To fix everything."

"Penny. We're here to focus on Liam. That's why I agreed to come to Newark. That's the only reason. The doctors here are going to fix him. And then we're going to go home. The four of us can be together."

"I don't understand what you're saying. You said you need surgery. So we have to make that…"

"And I can't have it right now. We just have to wait."

"For what?"

He just stared at me and shook his head.

I knelt down next to him again. "For what, James?"

"I'm sorry. I'm so sorry."

"You're…you…" I couldn't say the words. "No."

Now he was the one holding my face, trying to get me to look at him. To understand the unspeakable.

"No, no, no."

"Look at me," he said. "I'm right here. Right now. We still have time."

I lifted my eyes to his. "You can't." I couldn't make myself say it. "You can't."

"Baby, I care more about you than I care about life itself."

I shook my head. "Don't say that."

"It's true." He wiped away my tears with his thumbs. "We can enjoy whatever time we have. The four of us. It's what you asked for."

"I never asked for this. All I want is you. All I've ever wanted was you."

"And you'll always have a piece of me. In Scarlett. In Liam. They'll be there even if I'm not."

He's dying. I finally let myself think the word. Death. It rolled around in my head. Death was not an option. It felt like there was a knife in my chest. Nothing was more painful than a short life.

I was wrong before. He wasn't the one that was breaking. I was. I had just gotten my life back. I had just remembered what we had. Only to have it ripped away from me?

No. *Hell no.* My husband was not going to die. My son was not going to die. Nothing was going to strip me of this life I had fought so hard to get back. That *we* had fought so hard for in the first place. *No.* "No."

"Penny, it's not just something you can choose not to accept..."

"Yes it is. I don't accept it." Earlier tonight made so much more sense. He wasn't talking about an affair at Grottos. He was trying to tell me that he wasn't well. But James was not dying. I wouldn't allow it.

"Baby..."

"This is not our fate. We're going to grow old together. We're going to be sitting on some porch in rocking chairs with all our grandchildren surrounding us. That's our fate. I'm sorry you've had to face all of this on your own. But you're not on your own anymore. I'm right here. I'm going to take care of you."

He shook his head.

"The best cardiologist in the U.S. is coming to see you tomorrow. That whack-job in New York? He didn't have the answers. He didn't even know that I was being poisoned."

"No one knew you were being poisoned."

"Scarlett did. And she's not even four. Our doctors were basically toddlers."

He sighed and pulled me to his chest. "You can't just will my heart to heal."

"Do you wanna bet?"

He laughed. "No, I don't want to make a bet. I want you to be right."

"I'm right. I know I'm right." I listened to his heartbeat. Earlier today I had thought it was so steady. A few hours could change so much. I squeezed my eyes shut and focused on its thumping. The doctors were wrong. There was nothing wrong with James' heart. Someone who loved so hard couldn't possibly have a broken heart.

CHAPTER 16
Wednesday - *James*

I watched Penny breathing peacefully in her sleep. I knew she hadn't fallen asleep until recently because I hadn't been sleeping either. It felt like her eyes had bore into my soul all night long. Like she was afraid I'd slip away if she closed her eyes.

I stared at her shining hair on the pillow and the slope of her neck. The freckles beneath her blonde lashes. She hated how invisible her eyebrows and eyelashes were without makeup. But God was she beautiful. Just like this. The soft morning light streaming through the blinds cast shadows that heightened her features. Perfect.

I swallowed down the lump rising in my throat. I'd wanted to be strong for her and I had fallen apart. But the way she looked at me last night didn't make me feel weak. It made me feel like there was still hope. I knew that hope was a dangerous thing. I knew how much hope could hurt when things turned south. And it was hard enough hoping for our son to get better. How could we possibly hold out even more hope?

I had seen the look on my doctor's face when he went over my results. And for weeks, I had just ignored it. I thought the physical therapy would help. And I had other more important things on my mind. The health of my wife and child. I hadn't really faced the possibility that I was about to lose everything until last night. It felt so real. With our skin pressed together and our breaths intertwining, I could easily picture that mine would be gone. And she'd be alone. I'd leave her all alone.

She moaned softly in her sleep, her lips parting with each little breath.

Penny didn't deserve a life alone. And the thought of her being with another man made my stomach turn over. She couldn't be alone. And she couldn't be with someone else. So that meant I had to figure this out. There had to be a solution I hadn't thought of.

Penny made another moaning noise.

I reached out and tucked a strand of hair behind her ear. It was impossible not to touch her. It was like her body had a gravitational pull on my hand.

She slowly opened up her eyes. "Hey."

"Hey." I let my hand slide down her neck.

She shifted closer to me. "It's weird being back here, right? Where we first started?" She didn't say it, but I heard, "and where we might end?" in her silence.

I shook away the thought. "Do you miss it?"

"No." She sighed and closed her eyes again. "All I need is you. I'd go anywhere for you." She reached out and put her hand against my chest. Her eyebrows lowered slightly in concentration.

"What are you thinking?"

She opened her eyes. "I'm wishing. But I don't think it's necessary. It's going to be a good day. I can tell." Her fingers slowly trailed across my chest, lightly touching my scars, and stopped on the side of my ribcage. "I saw these the other day." She traced my tattoo with her thumb. "At the time I didn't remember that it had been just me. I should have at least put together the fact that the Liam one was new." She looked back up at me. "When did you add Scarlett and Liam?"

"My beautiful wife mentioned that my heart beats for my whole family now. You had asked me to add Scarlett awhile ago. And when you were unconscious…it was the one thing I could think of that I hadn't given you that you wanted. I thought that maybe if I made good on my promises you'd come back to me."

"You thought I wasn't waking up because I was mad at you?"

"It was a hard two weeks."

"I'll always come back to you." She nestled into my chest. "And you added Liam too." There was an awkward pause. "What if he doesn't make it?"

"What happened to your high hopes?"

"I think sometimes when you spread out your hope all of it feels a little fleeting." She took a deep breath. "A good night's sleep would have helped to recharge my positivity reserves, but I couldn't fall asleep."

"Me either." I ran my hand up and down her back. "Liam will always be a part of this family. No matter how long he's with us."

She tilted her head up and kissed beneath my chin. "I like the new tattoos. Always desecrating your perfect body." She kissed me again. "Thank you."

I held her tightly against my chest.

"We should get going. Liam's results will be in soon."

"You have no idea what time it is." I kissed the top of her head, not letting her move an inch.

"The sun is up. If the sun is up, that means we get the results soon." She squirmed in my embrace.

"It's barely 6 a.m. and Dr. Hughes said he wouldn't be in until 10."

"Then we can wait at the hospital. Just in case he comes early." She ducked out of my arms and shoved the blankets off of us. My t-shirt that she had worn to bed rose up her legs, showing just enough of her ass to make me forget what we had even been talking about.

"I think we could both use a distraction," I said.

She laughed as I dragged her back down onto the bed, pinning her in place just where I wanted her. She looked up at me with that smile I loved so much. Her hair cascaded over the pillow in pure perfection as she pretended to push me away again.

"How did I get so lucky?"

She winked. "By breaking all the rules."

I felt like I had been carrying the weight of the world on my shoulders for weeks. Now that I had Penny back in my arms? Anything was possible. But first, I was pretty sure she was asking me to break a few rules. Our house had always been pretty lawless though. So she'd have to suffice with a tickle war that would definitely end with us both naked on the floor.

She broke into a fit of giggles before my hand even reached under her arm.

"Don't even think about it!" She tried to squirm out of my grip again. But she wasn't going anywhere this time. She was all mine. Her heart. Her soul. Even her armpit.

***

Penny's leg bounced up and down as we waited in Dr. Hughes' office. I placed my hand on top of it so that she'd stop, but she proceeded to bounce her knee up and down, moving me with it.

"It's five after ten," she said. "Do you think that means something's wrong?"

I squeezed her knee, but that still didn't stop her. "No, he's a busy doctor in a busy hospital. That's why he couldn't come to New York, right? His schedule wouldn't allow it?"

"Right." She finally stopped bouncing her knee.

I wanted to distract her. I reached into my pocket and felt her engagement ring and wedding band. But not with that. This wasn't the time or place for a proposal. Instead, I reached into my other pocket and pulled out her cell phone. "I meant to give this back to you a while ago. I should have given it to you right away. I was just worried that you might try to reach out to someone you knew from your past instead of trying to connect with me." I handed it to her.

"You probably made the right call. I was so scared of you." She shook her head. "Scared is probably the wrong word. I was more intimidated than anything. And confused about how someone like you could end up with someone like me."

You could do it now. I could get down on one knee and put a smile on her face instead of a frown. I could distract her from our fears. But it just didn't feel right still. Not like this. "You mean someone truly and utterly perfect for me? It was an easy decision."

Her cheeks turned red. "I don't know how you did all these doctor check-ins by yourself while I was unconscious," she said, trying to subtly change the subject, but failing completely. "I don't think I could stand it."

"I usually didn't. Rob or my dad came to a lot of them with me. Liam and I were rarely ever alone in the hospital. With all our family and friends visiting you and him, I'm surprised there were ever any empty seats in the waiting room."

She smiled, but her lips were pressed tightly together. "I can't believe I didn't remember everyone. How empty my life would have been."

"But you did remember."

"I still need to apologize to everyone. Especially about trying to run away."

"Penny, it's okay. You're here now. That's all that matters."

"I wish Dr. Hughes was here right now too."

I laughed. "Don't make me tickle you again."

"You wouldn't dare."

I raised my eyebrow. "Wouldn't I though?"

She smiled, genuinely this time. "I love when you do that." She reached up and ran her index finger across my left eyebrow. "It's sinful what that does to me."

It seemed an awful lot like she was the one trying to distract me now. Before I could think of how I could actually make it sinful, the door behind us opened.

A nurse walked in. "I'm so sorry, but two of Dr. Hughes' patients just went into labor. There was a full moon last night so we've been pretty busy. It'll be a little while before he's able to sit down with the two of you…"

"Do you have the results of the tests?" Penny asked. She was staring at the notebook in the nurse's hand.

"Oh, no. I'm not the one to deliver news. Dr. Hughes wants to do that personally. And he'll be able to sit down with you shortly. Maybe in an hour or so. But in the meantime, we do have an exam room set up for you, Mr. Hunter. Dr. Young will be arriving any minute and we need to get all your tests done. We didn't expect his early arrival so we need to get started as soon as possible." She laughed nervously and checked her watch.

"Tests?" I asked. "I was under the impression that we were just going to go over my options."

The nurse shook her head. "No, he wants to run an EKG, echocardiogram, and a full stress test. So…we should get started." She opened the door for me.

"Is it okay if I come too?" Penny asked as we both stood up.

"If that's alright with you, Mr. Hunter," the nurse said.

"Of course." I grabbed Penny's hand and we followed the nurse out of the office and down the hall. All night and all morning we had been waiting for Liam's results. My thoughts were far away from my own problems. I could only focus on one issue at a time. Which was probably why I hadn't made a decision about what to do with my heart. I was waiting to hear if Liam was going to be okay. For weeks I had done nothing but wait. I had tried to ignore it, hoping that if I did the problem would just go away. But pretending it was getting stronger hadn't helped. Nothing had helped.

The nurse opened up a door and stopped so abruptly that Penny and I almost ran into her.

"Excuse me sir, but you can't be in here," she said.

I peered over her shoulder to see a man in jeans and a plaid shirt fooling with the settings on a treadmill in the corner. He cleared his throat and turned around. His long white beard almost reached his pants.

"Hello," he said in a cheery voice. "I'm Dr. Young. Come in, come in. We should get started."

He was quite rotund for a cardiologist. It looked like the suspenders he was wearing were actually necessary and not just a hipster fashion statement. He practically looked the way Santa Claus was depicted. He was the best cardiologist in the states? Was Penny serious about this? And why was he dressed like he was in a cabin up north? I thought Penny said he had been on vacation in Miami.

"Oh." The nurse didn't move. "You're Dr. Young?" She seemed as confused as me.

But I guess Penny recognized him from her research because she rushed into the room. "Thank you so much for agreeing to meet us here."

He clasped her outstretched hand between both of his. "No problem, dear. I'm happy to help."

The nurse walked into the room. "It'll take me about 45 minutes to run all the tests you required. If you'd like to get changed in the staff lounge..."

I almost laughed, but bit my tongue. Clearly I wasn't the only one alarmed by his appearance.

"Nonsense," Dr. Young said. "I'll just do the tests myself."

"Are you sure? I already have everything set up and..."

"Of course I'm sure," he said with a laugh. "These folks have requested to see me. I'll give them all my time. There's nothing else I need to do in Delaware. Such a quaint little town."

I was pretty sure he lived in the middle of the woods in a log cabin, so I had no idea why he thought Newark was so quaint.

"Did you want me to at least grab you a lab coat?" the nurse asked. "Or...a stethoscope maybe?"

"Nope. I have it right here." He reached into one of the pockets in his jeans, pulled a stethoscope out, blew on it, and wiped it on his flannel shirt. "Good as new."

What the hell? Who was this lunatic?

"Okay then. I'll just leave you to it. Page me if you need any assistance. The EKG machine is pretty new and..."

"We're good." He shooed her away. "Come in, Mr. Hunter. Let's get to the bottom of what's happening in that chest of yours. Just give me a minute to figure out this…oh…never mind, it's already on." He squirted a big glob of that jelly stuff used for echos onto the ground. "Warmer is on. Nothing worse than that being spread on you when it's cold. This warmer is the best development in the cardiology field in a decade." He chuckled to himself.

Really? The best development in a decade? "Penny, can I talk to you for a minute?" I asked and glared at her. She had to be kidding with this. My cardiologist in New York City was more competent than this old lumberjack.

"Can't it wait?" she asked. "James, he's flown all the way here."

"It's important."

"Nothing is as important as the health of your heart," Dr. Young said. "Well, besides for the health of your brain maybe. Mental health I mean. You both seem pretty good there though. Quick as a whip. You should take off your shirt."

I shook my head.

"James, take off your shirt," Penny said. Her voice was so stern that there was no room to argue.

If being examined by this lunatic was going to put her mind at east, then fine. But I wasn't going to listen to anything he had to say. He was a whack job. Hopefully Liam's doctor was actually good. We had met him last night and he at least acted and looked normal. Now I wasn't so sure. Maybe Penny had accidentally looked at a list of doctors recently diagnosed with insanity.

I pulled my shirt off and went over to the exam table that Dr. Young was patting way too enthusiastically.

"Great, now just lie back. We're going to do the EKG first so that the gel has more time to warm up. Don't want to send your whole body into shock." He took my shirt from my hand and tossed it toward Penny. It made it only halfway there and landed on the floor.

This guy was bad at everything. I slowly lay down and he started attaching the little stickers and wires all over my chest. I'd had plenty of EKG's done and they usually went just like this. At least he seemed like he knew what he was doing here. But when he leaned over to attach a few of the wires his long beard tickled my skin, throwing any confidence I had in him out the window.

"What do you do when you have a surgery?" I asked and nodded to his beard.

"Oh. I tuck it into my shirt." He dropped the rest of the cords down on top of me and proceeded to unbutton the top of his shirt.

"You don't have to…"

"No, it's fine. I should have done it earlier, it's just strange to introduce yourself with tucked beard, you see." He shoved his whole beard into his flannel shirt and then re-buttoned it to en-sure that everything would stay in place. "Better?"

"Sure." I tried for it to not come out as a question, but I couldn't help it. In a way, I did understand what he said. Intro-ducing yourself with your beard tucked into your shirt would be a ridiculous thing to do. But at the same time, ever doing it in the first place was probably more ridiculous. Tucked beard really shouldn't be a phrase ever used by anyone.

"Let's just finish this up." He attached the last few wires and turned on the machine beside him. He watched it for a few sec-onds before turning back to me. "Can you take a few deep, slow breaths for me?"

I closed my eyes and inhaled slowly before exhaling. For some reason, it caused me to yawn.

"Keep doing that for me."

"What? Yawning?"

"No, silly." He patted my shoulder like he had been patting the exam table a few minutes ago. "The deep breathing. Try to relax."

Relax? Yeah right. How was I supposed to relax when I was more worried about Liam and Penny's health than my own? I hadn't even agreed to this test. I had come here for Liam. And Penny should have been on this table instead of me. I wanted to know how her heart murmur was.

"Hmmm. Well. Okay then." He switched off the machine and started pulling off the stickers.

The words that had just come out of his mouth weren't at all comforting. But before I could ask him a question, he started talking again.

"Does that hurt?" He pulled another sticker off a little faster. "I never remember whether I should go slow or fast."

"It doesn't hurt."

"Fast it is then." He pulled off the rest of the stickers.

"So...how were the results?" I asked.

"Fine. Not great, but fine. Your heart is functioning normally which is good. But I might have been wrong about your brain."

"Excuse me?"

He tapped the side of my head. "I told you to take a few deep breaths. And you only gave me one medium breath. I should have taken your vitals before I wasted my time with a fast-breathing EKG." He wiped his stethoscope off on the front of his plaid shirt again and then pressed the dirty thing to my chest.

"I was taking deep breaths."

"No, you were most certainly not. Try it again for me."

I breathed in slow and exhaled even slower. Then another. And another.

"Medium. Medium. Medium." He looked so disappointed in me. "Are you stressed out about something?"

"Of course I'm stressed out." I swiped his stethoscope away from me. "My wife was in a coma for weeks and then didn't remember me when she woke up. My son was born too early and can't breathe without all these machines attached to him. We don't even know if we'll ever be able to bring him home."

"And your heart. You're worried about your heart."

"And my wife's heart."

"Oh, why didn't you say so? I can tell you whether or not you need to worry about that. Penny, dear. Come over here too, will you?" He fiddled with his pager as Penny joined us at the exam table. She didn't look weirded out at all by Dr. Young's tucked beard or enthusiastic table patting. She sat down next to me and whispered in my ear while Dr. Young was still playing with his pager. "Medium breaths, huh?"

"Medium breaths aren't a thing."

"James, you need to relax," she said. "Remember when I almost lost you before? That doctor warned you about your stress levels."

"I can't get this thing to work." Dr. Young tossed the pager down onto the floor. "Excuse me real quick." He walked out of the room without looking at either of us. Before the door swung closed, he yelled, "I need Penny Hunter's medical records!"

I laughed. "You want me to relax around that psychopath? Seriously, where did you find this guy?"

"He's the best of the best. And the best sometimes means…eccentric. Besides, what does it matter how he looks? He knows what he's doing."

"Are you sure about that?"

"Positive. He knew you were stressed out."

"Anyone can tell that I'm stressed out. Penny, I've been going through all of this on my own and I didn't have time to think about myself when..."

"You're not alone anymore. I'm right here. You do this thing where you carry the weight of the world on your shoulders. But I'm right here. I can carry some of it for you."

I smiled down at her. "I know. It's easier now that you're *you* again. But I just...how am I supposed to relax at a time like this? Any minute now Dr. Hughes will be available to discuss Liam's future. It's all I can think about. And you. You brought me here to focus on my health and I'm way more concerned about yours."

She shook her head. "You're worried about me? James, you don't have to worry about me. I'm fine. Please, please stop worrying about me." She placed her hand on my chest. "I need you to think about yourself for once. I need your heart to keep beating. I can't lose you. I just got you back." She shook her head. "I mean, I know I already had you...but I wasn't myself and..."

"I know. I get it." I grabbed her hand and held it in mine. "So what do you suggest I do to relax?"

"Pretend we're at the beach." She smiled at me hopefully.

I laughed. "The beach, huh?"

"Yeah. Pretend we're at the beach with Liam and Scarlett. And everyone else too. Rob, Daphne, and Soph. Mason and Bee, Melissa and Josh, Tyler and Hails, and Matt. Jen and Ian and our parents."

"I can't imagine my mother on a family vacation."

"Yup, she's there too. Smiling and laughing. Everyone's happy and healthy."

I took a deep breath. "That does sound nice. Maybe we can plan a vacation soon."

"Sooner rather than later." She rested her head on my shoulder. "What am I going to do with you?"

I ran my hand up and down her back. "I'll try harder to relax."

"Having to try hard to relax sounds unrelaxing."

I took a deep breath, concentrating on going slowly. "I don't know…maybe I'll take up meditation."

"And yoga."

"*And* yoga? Now you're just being greedy, woman."

She laughed. "We can do it together. I've always thought you'd look amazing in a pair of spandex shorts."

"Naked yoga sounds more appealing to me."

She laughed again, and I realized that was the sound that relaxed me the most. Of anything in the world, her laughter calmed me best. I took a slower breath this time. "Your laughter relaxes me."

She immediately sat up straighter and stared at me. "I've been stressed out. All of this…" she shook her head. "I was so focused on myself and being scared of you and what we had. I made all of this worse. And even before the accident I wasn't really myself. I was worried about the baby and my heart. I was so consumed with my own thoughts and fears that I didn't realize the effect that my reactions had on you…"

"That wasn't what I was saying." I squeezed her hand. "I just meant that I love seeing you smile and laugh. I want to hear your laughter more often from here on out, that's all. This has been stressful for everyone. It's no one's fault. Well, I guess technically it is. And Dr. Nelson is going to pay for his crimes. But it's certainly not your fault."

"I could have made it easier."

"You didn't know who I was. Penny." I grabbed the bottom of her chin and tilted her head toward mine. "Beating yourself up about what happened is the last thing in the world I want. I just want us to go back to the way things were. When we were both so happy that it seemed like we were in this impenetrable bubble."

Dr. Young cleared his throat from behind us.

Penny's chin dropped from my hand when she pulled away from me.

"I have all the records right here!" the doctor said. "Sorry it took me so long. All the nurses here are very unresponsive to doctors' requests."

I didn't have the heart to tell him it was because no one in their right mind would believe he was a doctor.

"And faxing is one of the greatest inventions of all time, but I do wish there was something a little faster, don't you?"

I just stared at him. Had he never heard of the internet?

"So let's see…Penny, Penny, Penny." He flipped through the pages in the file. "Your heart isn't of concern at all. There is just a teensy tiny murmur." He walked back and forth while he looked at the pages. "One of your valves leaks, and it may have been slightly worse when you were pregnant, but it should be back to normal now. Let's have a look-see." He pulled out his stethoscope and pressed it against her chest. "Take a deep breath for me."

Penny followed his instructions.

"Your wife knows how to breathe properly," he said and stuffed his stethoscope back in his pocket. "I could barely even hear the tiny little squeak the murmur makes. This is nothing to worry about, James."

"See," Penny said with a smile. "You don't have to worry about me."

"There are tons of people out there that have the same size murmur and will never know. You need a special ear to hear the squeak." He pointed to his own ear. "I hear squeaks all the time. Even in my sleep. But I have mice in my house." He laughed at his own joke. "But people with this size murmur don't have to worry what-so-ever. It's a nothing cardiovascular problem. It's what we in the biz call a nada cardio issue. I mean, you even went through a major surgery and nothing happened with your heart." He glanced down at the pages. "A bilateral oophorectomy. It's been a while since I've been in medical school, but unilateral definitely means one. Bilateral would be two. So..." he shook his head back and forth as he thought. "You had both ovaries and both fallopian tubes removed."

I had wanted to get a second opinion on her bilateral oophorectomy. She had only heard it from some random doctor that didn't know her records. How could he possibly know without opening her up? I kept thinking that to myself over and over. But here it was. Dr. Young had her records and he was confirming it.

"And I'm fine," Penny said. "See...there's nothing to worry about, James."

We locked eyes for just a moment. And I knew she had been holding out hope too. That maybe, just maybe that other doctor had been wrong.

"Maybe James' heart will beat a little slower if you're not in the room, Penny. Nothing like a young wife to get the mister's heart racing."

I wanted to punch him in the face.

"Yeah." Penny dropped her gaze from mine. "I'm going to go visit Liam while you two finish up, okay? Think of the beach." She squeezed my hand before hopping off the exam table.

I watched her duck out of the room as quickly as possible. And I hoped that telling her I loved her laughter didn't mean she felt like she couldn't cry around me. I knew she wanted more kids. Hell, if I was being honest with myself, *I* wanted more kids. But that wasn't going to happen for us.

"Deep breaths this time, okay?" Dr. Young said as he pulled his stethoscope back out.

But my mind was far away.

CHAPTER 17

Wednesday - *Penny*

I rushed out of the room before James could see me cry. He had just told me that my laughter was what reduced his stress. Yet, here I was.

I was trying to be strong. But my husband's heart was failing. My baby boy couldn't even breathe without being attached to all those machines. And the future I wanted had just disappeared. Really. There were no more ifs, ands, or buts about it. No more children. It was a fact now instead of just a...I shook away the thought. It had always been a fact. I had just let myself believe for no reason at all. I was so filled with hope for James and Liam that I let a little of that hope creep into my own situation as well.

My feet stopped moving and I leaned against the wall in some random hallway of the hospital. I couldn't go see Liam like this. I was trying so hard to hold it together and then one ounce of bad news had me teetering over the edge. I let myself cry as my back slid down the wall. My butt hit the floor with a thud and I pulled my knees into my chest. I needed to get all of this out of my system before James was done his exam. I needed to be a ball of positive energy filled with laughter and smiles and hope. The thought made me cry even harder. I felt like I was breaking under the stress that I just promised James I could help carry.

But it was more than that. I felt like something in my life was missing. Maybe it was the idea of the children I'd never have now. Like there was a part of me I didn't have anymore. Hopes and dreams, maybe. It certainly wasn't my phone. Having that back meant nothing to me. I hadn't missed it at all.

I leaned over more and felt the waistband of my shorts biting at my skin. God, and I was also fat. I hated the extra baby weight I had put on. Or maybe I just hated these short. Why did I pack jean shorts anyway? I was a grownup. Grownups didn't wear cutoff jean shorts.

Pull yourself together. I needed to find a way to stop crying. I needed to think of kittens or baby goats. Damn it, why did my go to happy place revolve solely around babies?

My phone started vibrating in my pocket. I pulled it out to see Rob's name. If anyone in the world could cheer me up, it was him. It felt like the universe had told him that I needed him right now. Maybe having my phone back was a good thing after all. I slid my finger across the screen.

"Hey," I said.

"I guess James finally gave you all your shit back?"

"Mhm."

"Did he give you your rings back in some elaborate over the top way? I told him it wasn't necessary. That you'd remember his original proposal soon enough."

I looked down at my left hand. The tan lines on my ring finger. Was that why I felt empty? Because James hadn't given me my rings back? I took a deep breath and closed my hand into a fist. It did feel off. It felt too light. Too meaningless. Why hadn't he given them back?

"Penny?"

I wasn't even sure what he had asked. "Yeah."

"Are you okay?"

I sniffed. "No. Not really."

"Fuck. It was bad news? Give it to me straight. Tell me everything. Let me put you on speaker phone so Daphne can hear too."

"No." I shook my head. "No, there's no news at all."

"Oh." There was an awkward pause. "Then what's wrong?"

This wasn't something I should talk about with Rob. It was a conversation I needed to have with James. But technically we'd already had it. He said he was okay that we couldn't have more children. That he wouldn't have wanted me to get pregnant again anyway because it was too risky. But I had seen the hope in his eyes for a minute there. That maybe. Just...maybe.

"It's nothing, Rob. How is Scarlett doing?"

"Scarlett's fine. Tell me what's wrong. I can tell that you've been crying, and you know that you suck at lying. So spill it."

I sniffed again. "My shorts don't fit."

"Try again."

I laughed. "They really don't. And I feel like I've had these since college. Maybe I'm more like that lost 19-year-old girl than I realize." I placed my forehead in my hand.

"Everything that's lost can be found."

"Even when it's your future?"

"What have you lost, Penny? You just got everything back."

I slid my legs out in front of me, not caring that I was in the way of anyone walking past. "Did James tell you about my surgery?"

"The C-section? No, he never mentioned it. We all assumed you had it."

"No, not that one. I had..." I let my voice trail off. "The name doesn't matter. I can't have any more children. I wanted more children. There's so much going on right here right now and I feel like what I was looking forward to most in the future isn't there anymore. And I just feel like...like I've been robbed."

"Robbed should be a good term don't you think? Like, damn girl, you just robbed the shit out of that."

I laughed. "That's not helping."

"You literally just laughed."

I laughed again.

"See!" He laughed too for a few seconds. And then the line went completely silent.

I didn't have anything to fill the silence. I let it stretch between us.

"I'm sorry, Penny," he finally said.

"Me too. I know James wanted more kids. He might say otherwise, but you should have seen his face when the doctor confirmed it." I looked down at my naked ring finger. "What if he wants that more than he wants me?"

"Kids? Are you kidding? I mean, he loves Scarlett and Liam. But he lives for you, Penny. He was a mess when you were unconscious. And that day you ran out on all of us? It nearly killed him."

"He hasn't given me my rings back."

"Oh."

"I'm trying not to read into that. But...he gave me back my phone."

"Well, like I said earlier, he wanted to do it in some grand way. He's probably just planning something over the top romantic."

"Or debating whether he wants to give them back to me at all. And it's more than just the kids. He said my laughter is what calms him down. And I've been this huge stress..."

"Monster. You've been a stress monster."

I laughed. "Is that what you're calling it?"

"Absolutely. You've been in quite the mood ever since you started submitting your manuscript to agents."

"I know. So add that on top of my inability to have children. And my fatness."

"Penny, you are a beautiful goddess."

"You're inappropriate."

"You're sexy."

"Rob…"

"You're a perfect 10."

"I don't know how Daphne isn't always mad at you."

"She understands me. Just like James understands you. And loves you. He's not going to divorce you, Penny. Not in a million years."

I ran my thumb along the tan line on my ring finger. *I hope you're right.* "Hey, you got me to stop crying."

"It was all my lines right? How about…your body is a wonderland?"

"I'm going to go hang out with Liam. He can't say inappropriate things yet."

"Silence is consent."

"Gross, Rob."

He laughed. "I love you, Penny. Cheer up, okay? We're planning a huge welcome home party for you guys. Bring back J.J. for us."

"His name is Liam." I stood up and brushed the dust off my ass.

"Whatever. Let me know when you're heading back. We might even hire your gay wedding planner to organize the event just to make James and Mason super uncomfortable. I'm still a little pissed that he never hit on me."

"You can't hire Justin. He only does weddings. Besides, you can't have all the men and all the women in New York fawning over you."

"Why not? What happened to freedom of...sex or whatever."

I laughed. "Bye, Rob."

"Bye, sweet-cheeks."

I slid the phone back into my pocket. Freedom of sex. Not the right terminology whatsoever. But it had given me an idea. I looked down at my empty ring finger. That was the part of me that was missing. I was used to wearing a ring to symbolize my love and devotion to James. I only saw one way to fix that. I needed to get my rings back.

I made my way down the hall to the NICU. The only problem with getting my rings back was that I didn't know how. *Should I just ask for them back? Should I propose?*

The nurse started unhooking Liam from tubes and machines when I walked in. After a few minutes, he was in my arms and for a moment I was able to forget about all my worries. He felt so comfortable in my arms. I hoped he felt as comforted by my presence as I did by his.

"What do you think, baby boy?" I whispered. "What should I do?"

He blinked up at me.

"If I propose, it needs to be the epitome of romance. Your dad always does these huge grand gestures. I want to do something like that for him."

He opened his tiny little mouth and yawned.

"Am I boring you?" I leaned down and kissed his forehead. "What would you do, Liam?"

He yawned again.

"It's easy for you. You'd propose beautifully. You'll be perfectly romantic just like your father." I smiled. *Just like your father.* "You're brilliant, Liam." I kissed his forehead again and looked up at the nurse in the room. "Do you know when Dr. Hughes is going to be done with his deliveries?"

"I haven't heard anything from him yet, so it'll still be awhile."

"If James comes, could you tell him I stepped out for a minute?"

"Where should I tell him you've gone?"

"If he's worried just...have him text me." I'd almost forgotten that I had my phone back. "I'll be back soon, baby boy." I rocked Liam in my arms once more. "Keep Daddy distracted okay?" I handed him over to the nurse and then ran out of the room.

CHAPTER 18
Wednesday - *James*

"Try the deep breathing again," Dr. Young said.

I concentrated as hard as I could. Inhale. Exhale. But I was thinking about Penny running out of the room. I needed to know if she was okay. I never should have let her leave.

Dr. Young sighed and removed the wand he had been moving around in the gel. The gel that was practically scalding when he had squirted it onto my chest.

"You're not good at this," he said.

"Good at what?"

"Breathing. Breathing, James. Your heart is functioning fine. The reason your cardiologist has been talking about another possible surgery is because you're going to reverse what your last surgery fixed in a matter of days at this rate. You need to calm down."

"I am calm," I said way too defensively for a calm person.

Dr. Young untucked his beard from his shirt. "And I'm a canary with a beard."

I knew he was trying to make a point. But I didn't find it funny at all. I sat up, ignoring the gel sliding down my chest.

"Your mind is getting in the way of your heart's health." He tapped the side of my head.

I pushed his hand away. "I'm gonna go try to find Penny."

"Not yet you aren't. Not till we get to the bottom of this. Come on. Hit me with more of your issues. We've been over your worries about your son and wife. What else do you got? I can take it. Canary can handle it." He grinned at me.

"I have a therapist."

"And for 22 more hours you also have me." He sat down beside me on the exam table. "Your wife paid me good money to come see you."

"I bet she did."

"Are you stressed about money?"

"No."

"I know hospital bills can add up, but..."

"I'm not stressed about money." It was basically the one thing I wasn't stressed about.

"If you keep going at this rate, you'll force my hand. I'll have to perform surgery. And your heart is still weak from your last one."

I shook my head.

"I'm good at what I do. But you'll die if we have to perform that surgery, James. You'll die."

"I don't know what you want me to say. I told you about my wife and child. I'm worried about both of them. That's it."

"Yet your heart is still racing. There's something else. Something else that is stressing you out."

"I'm not stressed! I'm angry." I could feel my heart racing just thinking about it.

Dr. Young nodded expectantly. "Good. And why are you angry?"

"Because I'm the one that fucked up when I was young. I was the one that got in fights and did drugs and got locked up. This bad karma that my family is experiencing is my fault. They didn't do anything to deserve any of this. It's all on me." *It's all on me.*

"Surely that was all a long time ago now. You're not such a young man anymore. And karma isn't real. You know that. That's not it either. Tell me why you're angry."

"I just told you."

"Try again."

I ran my fingers through my hair.

"Maybe it's not stress or anger. Maybe it's something else entirely."

I shook my head.

"I think you're scared, James. Scared of losing that beautiful wife of yours."

I shook my head again and pulled the rings out of my pocket. "I'm worried I already lost her." I turned the rings over in my palm.

"She gave those back to you?"

"No. The doctors took them off during her surgery. I've wanted to give them back to her. But at first she didn't remember who I was. And now...now she does."

"You're nervous. To propose a second time to your wife. Why? She already said yes."

"She was too young to know better. She's had years more experience now. She's lived with me. She's seen my ups and downs. She knows better now. And she hasn't made one hint that she wants them back. What if she doesn't want them back?"

"That woman in here that I saw? The one that talked to me on the phone for nearly an hour, begging me to come here to see you? That woman loves you, James." He lifted up his stethoscope and pressed it against my chest. "There. Now that's the deep breath I've been waiting for."

I laughed. *Did this lunatic actually just help me?*

"I don't think you believed me when I said it earlier, but karma really doesn't exist. We control what happens in our lives."

"I'm a believer in fate." Penny was such a believer in it that she had made me a believer too. "Karma. Fate. They must all be aligned somehow." I slid the rings back into my pocket.

"Oh, the fates are real. But karma shmarma. It's nonsensical. And you remember it." He patted the gel on my chest. "A few more days of this relaxed breathing and you'll be as good as new. I'll stay till the end of the week to monitor your progress. Free of charge because you've already paid me much more than a week's salary. But stick to this and there will be no issues. And certainly no surgery."

"Thank you." My words didn't feel like enough. This man had just told me what I needed to do to get my life back. I owed him everything.

"Here, let me clean you up." He grabbed a towel and ran it down my chest. "Oh my, what big abs you have."

I laughed.

"I'll fix your heart and you can show me how to get abs of steel. I can cut my beard if I have muscles like those to show off." He patted his beer belly.

"Deal, Dr. Young."

He grinned. "Call me Gooch. All my friends do."

"Gooch?"

"Yup. Like Gucci but oh so much less extra." He patted my cheek. "And I have no idea why. My first name is Simon. I'll see you tomorrow." He winked at me and left me alone in the exam room.

I slid off the table, wondering if all of that had been a strange dream. I grabbed my shirt off the floor and pulled it over my head. Breathe in. Breathe out. I needed two days to make sure my heart was healed up. Two days of no stress. I walked out of the room and wandered toward the NICU.

I wasn't sure how I was going to handle our meeting with Dr. Hughes. And I needed to talk to Penny about her surgery. I needed her to know that I was fine with the size of our family. But if she wanted it to grow, that there were other options besides having biological kids of our own. We'd figure something out together.

And as soon as I got the all clear from Dr. Young, I'd propose again. Until then, I couldn't think about it. I just needed to focus on breathing. I opened up the door of the NICU and stopped by my son. I got down close to the glass. "Hey, little dude. How are you feeling today?" He was sleeping peacefully.

"Did you want to hold him?"

I shook my head. "I don't want to disturb him while he's sleeping. Have you seen my wife?"

"Yes. She said she had to step out for a few minutes. But that you could text her if you needed anything. I did just hear from Dr. Hughes too. He's scrubbing off from a delivery. He should be coming up to meet you in about ten minutes. You can feel free to wait in his office."

"Great. Did Penny mention where she was going?"

She shook her head. "No. I'm sorry, she didn't say." She looked back down at her clipboard. "If you'll excuse me." She went over to one of the other babies and started to check his vitals.

"It's going to be good news, Liam," I said down to him sleeping. "I know it will be." I went back out into the hall and sent Penny a text letting her know Dr. Hughes would be ready in ten minutes. There was a very real part of me that wanted to freak out. To demand to know where she was so I could come get her. To ask her if she at least took Ian with her.

But I couldn't afford to do that. Not for at least two days. And if I was being honest with myself, I could never do it again. I was going to be here for my family. Always. I let myself back into Dr. Hughes' office and sat down where I had earlier this morning.

Instead of getting anxious waiting to hear back from Penny, or waiting for the news of Liam, I closed my eyes and pictured the beach. That perfect scene that Penny had painted for me earlier. *Breathe in. Breathe out.* I could picture it so clearly.

***

"Did waiting for me put you to sleep?"

I opened my eyes with a start. Dr. Hughes was standing by his desk. I shook my head trying to rid myself of my dreams, even though they had been perfect. It was the first time I'd really been able to picture my life outside the city. It felt right. Away from the people and chaos and stress. I shook my head again, having a hard time coming back to reality and the problems that still loomed before me. "I'm sorry. Yes, I must have fallen asleep."

"Nonsense, I'm the one that's sorry to have kept you waiting, Mr. Hunter. But I'm glad to see that you've found time to get rested up after your flight."

"It was a short flight," I said. "It's just been a long morning."

He nodded. "Will your wife be joining us?"

"Yeah, she should be here. One second." I glanced down at my phone. There was a text from her saying she'd be back soon. But that was from half an hour ago. I had taken quite a nap. And

I honestly couldn't remember the last time I had napped. Dr. Young had somehow taken away all my stress. I yawned. "She'll be here shortly."

"Great. Should we wait for her or…"

"How were the test results?" I said at the exact same time.

He chuckled.

"Is Liam going to be okay?" I knew I should wait for Penny, but I had been waiting weeks for good news when it came to my son. I wasn't sure I could wait any longer.

Dr. Hughes smiled as he sat down behind his desk. "Cutting right to the chase. I like the way you think, Mr. Hunter." He lifted up a folder and placed it on top of this desk. "The results were good. Very good actually." He didn't open up the folder. Like he knew the information forward and backward. Like he had actually taken the time to assess my son's health.

I had never felt that way in New York. Three doctors had been assigned to Liam in the city. And sometimes their opinions didn't even align on what steps to take next. It was almost like they had looked to me for the answers. I didn't have them. How could I possibly have them? I was barely staying afloat. My whole family had been falling apart and I hadn't had my wife by my side.

"What does very good mean, exactly?" I asked. "Do you have a pen and paper so I can write some things down? Penny usually carries those with her." I patted my pockets like the items I need-ed would just appear like they had for Dr. Young.

"I don't think there's anything to write down. I've run every test I could possibly think of," the doctor said. "I haven't been monitoring him since his birth, but from what I can tell from the documents sent over, he's making an impressive recovery. And I saw that your wife's records were sent over this morning. I glanced at them and I believe that she must have suffered most of the consequences from the poison. I don't see any traces of it in Liam. And it doesn't appear to be affecting his vitals or organs in any way. Yes, he was born early, but many babies are. He only has symptoms related to being born early, not from anything else. He's going to be alright."

It sounded too good to be true. *How?* After everything...how? I shook my head. "But the doctors in New York talked about possible disabilities down the road. That his mental development may be affected. That my son would never have a normal life."

"I have no reason to see why that would happen. There are zero signs that he's not developing properly. His lungs are the only issue that I can see, and as I said, that's only a symptom from his early birth. I'm actually going to advise that we take him off his CPAP machine at the end of the week if he keeps progressing this well."

"What does that mean?" Penny asked from behind us. "He's able to breathe on his own now? Without any machines?" She rushed into the room. "I'm sorry I'm late," she squeezed my shoulder.

"It means you'll be able to take him home. You'll be able to take your perfectly healthy baby boy home this weekend."

A sob escaped from Penny. "There's nothing wrong with him?"

"I don't believe there is. As I was telling your husband earlier, we've run every test we could think of. I think he's going to be just fine."

"Should you check your notes?" She gestured to his unopened notebook. "I don't...we were told he couldn't leave the hospital for another month."

IVY SMOAK

"Besides for those deliveries this morning I've been absorbed in this case and only this case since I got your call. Liam has had my full attention. The university appreciates your donations."

I shook my head. "How could the other doctors have been so wrong? I thought he was going to die. They made me believe he was going to die. I thought we were going to have to say goodbye to him before my wife even came out of her coma." I felt a tear run down my cheek and quickly brushed it away. "What changed?"

"They were too close to the problem. They were putting all their time and energy into the possibility of him being poisoned without really taking the time to study *him*. Also, Mrs. Hunter's gynecologist was associated with that hospital. They were probably concerned about covering themselves in case of a lawsuit. Saying the worst is yet to come all along protected them from a worst case scenario.

"And despite everything he's been through...I believe your son's a fighter. He's meant to be here. He truly has made a miraculous recovery. I'd let you take him home today, but I always like to be cautious. But Liam's going to be okay."

Liam's going to be okay. It felt like I could breathe again. This time without concentrating so hard on it. "Thank you." I stood up and outstretched my hand.

But before Dr. Hughes shook it, Penny practically tackled me in a hug.

"We're going to get to bring him home." I could barely understand her through her sobs. "He's going to make a full recovery." She pulled away from me. "A full recovery, right? That's what all that means?"

Dr. Hughes smiled. "I believe so."

"And he's the best in his field, James. The best. If he thinks Liam is fine, then Liam is fine." She let go of me and ran around the desk to hug Dr. Hughes. "Thank you. Thank you so much."

He laughed. "You're welcome."

I reached my hand out and this time he grasped it. "I don't know how we can ever thank you enough."

"It's my job. The days I get to deliver good news are the ones I live for. I'll give you two a minute." He left us alone in his office.

I turned to Penny. "I don't know if I should be jealous right now...you just said Dr. Hughes was the best and basically threw yourself into his arms. But I can't stop smiling."

"Liam's going to be okay." She wiped away her own tears, leaving nothing but a beautiful smile on her face.

"Our son's going to be okay!" I lifted her up and twirled around in a circle.

Her laughter filled the room, intertwining with my own. My son was going to live. And I was going to be there right next to him for as long as humanly possible. I wasn't going anywhere either. My son needed me. Who else was going to teach him how to throw a baseball? Or shave? Or tie a bowtie?

I let Penny's body slide back down the front of mine. "He's going to live." I nestled my face in her hair and held her as we both smiled. And cried. And laughed until it hurt.

CHAPTER 19
Wednesday - *Penny*

I could have stayed in James' arms for eternity and been perfectly happy. I kept laughing and sobbing and I couldn't seem to stabilize my emotions no matter how hard I tried.

"I know Dr. Hughes said donations. With an s. You're probably wondering about that. But I had to make another one of those to get us on his schedule. I think it was worth it. I know I should have asked you first. We usually make all our donation decisions together but..."

"Penny." He grabbed both sides of my face, forcing my eyes to meet his. "Our son's going to be okay. He's going to live a long, healthy, normal life. There is no price I wouldn't have been willing to pay to hear those words."

And then I was crying again.

He ran his thumbs beneath my eyes to remove my tears. "I think we should go see him. Don't you?"

"You mean our healthy, beautiful, perfect baby boy that we get to bring home in two days?"

"That's the one."

"I'm so glad we have one of those now. I mean...I knew he was beautiful and perfect. He looks just like you. But now he's healthy too." I stood on my tiptoes to kiss him, but he met me halfway. I melted into him. I was ecstatic. Thrilled. Completely over-the-moon. But my stress hadn't been cut in half. My nerves hadn't been sliced in two. It had all just attached itself to James. And now all my worries and fears could be focused. All my hope too. I knew he'd have results from his tests now. But I needed a minute to be joyous. Just one minute where it felt like everything was okay.

"He has your eyes though," James said, pulling me out of my thoughts. "When you were unconscious and I couldn't look into your eyes, I saw so much of you in him. And he makes the same noises as you do when you sleep. These adorable little moans."

I laughed. "I don't make noises when I sleep."

He made a face that very much made it seem like he disagreed with me.

"I do not." I lightly shoved his shoulder.

He grabbed my hand and pulled me to the door. "Let's go see that healthy, beautiful, perfect baby boy we made."

I almost felt like a teenager as we walked hand-in-hand through the hospital. Joking around with James. Laughing. For just one little moment, my thoughts were all as light as air. And just thinking it made me feel guilty. It wasn't fair for my thoughts to be as light as air when James' were still heavy.

I stopped him outside of the NICU. "I love being this happy."

"And I love when you're happy."

I searched his eyes. "Tell me. Tell me everything. Just rip the Band-Aid off. Don't let me start guessing until I come to some wild conclusion like you cheated on me and I end up..." I glanced around the hospital, "throwing a full bedpan at you."

James laughed. "We're escalating to flinging poo now?"

"I'm being serious." I stepped closer to him, trying to ignore the busy hallway. "I can tell you thought Dr. Young was crazy. I get it, he looked crazy and acted crazy, but he's brilliant in his field. You have to tell me what he said. I can't take another second of suspense."

He reached out and tucked a loose strand of hair behind my ear. "He thinks if I take it easy the next few days that my heart will have time to heal. And he thinks if it heals properly, there's no reason why I should need surgery. Ever."

I nodded. "Ever?"

"Ever."

I squealed and threw my arms around him. "I feel like I'm so full of good news I could burst. We need to call everyone and tell them. And we need to go see Liam. And…"

He grabbed the back of my neck and pulled me into a soul crushing kiss. He felt whole. And strong. And so much himself again. I gripped the front of his shirt, deepening the kiss until I was practically moaning.

"We need to find a way to alleviate your stress," I said when I finally willed myself to pull away. "Maybe I'll give in to the naked yoga thing."

"Let's take the next two days really slowly."

"Slow motion." I nodded. "I. Got. It."

James laughed. "You don't have to speak slowly. But…let's just hang out here and be happy. Let's be young and in love in Newark, Delaware."

"That's easy. We don't even have to play make-believe. That's just what we are." I stood on my tiptoes and kissed him again. "We get to bring Liam home."

"One big, healthy family."

"Happy too."

He ran his hand down the side of my neck. "I hope you're happy, Penny."

"Are you kidding? I've never been so happy in my entire life." I pressed the side of my face against his chest. Nothing could have been better than this moment.

***

I turned off the movie when the credits started rolling and turned to James. "So? What did you think?"

"It was funny."

My feet were resting in his lap, so I gently kicked his thigh. "What do you mean it was funny?"

"It is a comedy, right? I'm pretty sure that's what it's listed as." He set down his slice of pizza, like he was ready to prove his point. Instead of continuing though, he just stared at me. Waiting patiently to understand the importance of this romance.

"Yes, a romantic comedy. But what did you think about the whole meaning of their relationship?"

He stared at me skeptically. "I thought Westley looked an awful lot like Tyler. It was hard to look past that."

I laughed. "They don't look that similar. Just like the…hair and eyes. But James, it isn't about what he looks like. That has absolutely nothing to do with it."

"Then I don't get it."

I rolled my eyes. Sometimes men were so dense. "I first saw this movie when I was a freshman in high school I think. And I kept hoping that one day, someone would love me that much. But in my heart, I thought I knew that would never be the case. Because no one had ever loved me. No one had ever put me first. I didn't know how that felt. I thought I was destined to be alone. Until you."

He grabbed my ankle and pulled me closer to him on the couch. "I love you that much."

"I know. I love you that much too. Which reminds me...I did something. You've probably been wondering where I disappeared to earlier today?"

"I was wondering. But my decision to have zero stress in my life told me to ignore it. That you'd tell me when you were ready."

"I'm ready."

"And this isn't going to stress me out?"

"Not in the slightest. At least, I hope not. I guess if you don't like it..." I shook my head. "You'll like it."

He raised his eyebrow in that sexy way of his.

I moved my feet off his lap and stood up. He was watching me so expectantly. Like I truly did hold the key to his heart. Like every move I made he wanted to see and be there with me. Like he loved me more than any hero in any movie. I slowly pulled my shirt off over my head.

"I feel like I'm going to like this."

I laughed and tossed my shirt at him.

He caught it before it covered his head. "A striptease to celebrate the health of our family?"

"Well, it can turn into that if you want. But I need to show you something first." I unhooked my bra and pulled it off.

His eyes were glued to my breasts.

"James." I waved my hand in front of his face. "I'm trying to show you something." I pointed to the bandage on the side of my ribcage. I tried not to wince as I pulled it off.

I watched his eyes scan the words. And the lines of an EKG machine. And the date that we first met.

"My heart beats for you," he said slowly.

I couldn't read his expression at all. "The one you got was the most romantic thing in the world. I know I couldn't compete with you writing, 'my life began the day I met you,' on the side of your ribcage. But I want you to know that you're never alone, James. That even though you're there to catch me when I fall, I'm there to catch you too. You know? And when life gets hard and it feels like you have the weight of the world on your shoulders, I'm there to carry some of that weight for you. Forever and always."

He leaned forward and lightly traced the skin beneath my tattoo. "You got a tattoo for me."

"I did. I needed you to know how much I cared. I didn't know how else to show you."

"You desecrated your perfect body for me?" He finally lifted his gaze off the words and locked eyes with me.

I smiled. "I said those exact words to you on our wedding day."

"I'll never forget them."

"But I liked yours. I meant the desecrate thing playfully. I love yours actually." There was an awkward silence. "Please tell me you don't hate it."

"I don't hate it."

"But you don't like it?"

"I think that you're missing two dates." He smiled up at me.

I laughed and put my hands on my hips. "This thing hurt like hell. If I had known that, I wouldn't have pressured you into getting the other two dates."

"I love it, Penny."

"Really?"

"Yes, really."

"So…that brings me to my next point. Can I please have my rings back? I feel like since you've been wearing yours and I don't have mine that people think I'm your mistress or something. I don't want there to be any more rumors about us ever again. And technically those are mine. You gave them to me." I held out my hand out so he could place them in my palm.

"I've thought of a lot of ways to do this. Most of them didn't involve you standing topless in front of me."

"Oh. I can put…"

"No, this is a lot better than I ever imagined it."

I smiled at him.

He scooted off the couch and got down on one knee in front of me. "I was going to wait until the end of the week to do this right. Let myself be stressed out and everything over your response. But you've made it pretty clear what your answer is going to be."

I could feel tears welling in my eyes.

"I love you with all my heart. With every ounce of my being. And I don't need to do this in the coffee shop. I don't need to recreate the past. Our story was great. But our future is only just beginning. And I'm not going anywhere. No matter what life throws at us, all I know is that I want you by my side. You said it best. My heart beats for you." He reached into his pocket and pulled out my rings. "Penny, will you do me the honor of continuing to be my wife?"

"A million times yes."

He pulled me down into his arms.

"I've experienced life without you and it was a life not worth living," I said as I nuzzled my face against his neck. "I don't know how I ever forgot you because everything about you is unforgettable. I'll love you until the day I die, way way in the future."

I leaned back so he could slide my rings back where they belonged. I'd never take them off again. They were beautiful. And they were mine. We were finally back where we were supposed to be.

He captured my lips in a kiss that had my head spinning.

"Normally I'd pick you up and carry you to the bed, but I'm doing my best to follow the doctor's orders."

I laughed and looked behind me. "Well, how many times do you think Rob had sex on this couch?"

James made a gagging noise. "I don't want to think about that."

I laughed. "Me either." I looked down at the fabric. "It's been cleaned, right?"

He pulled me back into a kiss, pushing aside any thoughts I had of dirty couches.

Who the hell cared when the hottest guy on earth was right in front of them? I was pretty sure I could make love to him even if we were in a disgusting bathroom in a dingy bar. "I don't care if it's dirty," I said and pulled on the front of his shirt so he'd follow me back up to the couch. "We're about to make it dirtier, anyway."

"God I love you."

We fell together in a tangle of limbs onto the couch. I wanted a million more of these moments. Skin against skin. Sinful things whispered in my ear. I loved James Hunter. I loved him more than life itself. All the ups and downs brought me to one conclusion every single time. I loved this man. Whether he was my professor, boyfriend, fiancé, boss, or husband. I loved him in every single form. He was my everything. And my heart truly did beat for him.

CHAPTER 20
Friday - *Penny*

Our few days in Newark had flown by. I had never been more in love with the man beside me. I was so blissfully happy. James and Liam had both been given the all-clear. We were going home today.

It felt like we were back where we started. Despite the changes around campus. I pulled James toward the strange new statue I had seen last time I was here.

"And this," I said. "What the heck is this?" I gestured to the hideous thing.

"You don't like change very much."

"I don't mind change if it makes any sense at all. But this thing ruined the aesthetic of this circle. Remember how you could go to the center and clap and it would echo?"

James shoved his hands into his pockets as he watched me examine the statue. "No, I wasn't aware of that."

I looked back up at him. "What kind of professor were you?"

He smiled in that seductive way of his. "A bad one."

I walked back over to him. "You were a great professor. With a bad habit of seducing students."

"Student. Not plural."

"See. You were a good professor. And you still are back home. Let me see if it still echoes." I looked over my shoulder to see if anyone was coming before I proceeded to climb up onto the concrete book.

James laughed as I started clapping in the center of the book.

"Am I centered? Or is over here better?" I stepped to the side and started clapping again.

James started laughing even harder.

"Why are you laughing at me?"

"Because you look like a lunatic."

I stuck my tongue out at him and looked back down at the statue I was standing on. "It doesn't echo back. This stupid statue ruined everything."

"Everything?"

"Fine, not everything." I let James help me down from the hideous monstrosity. "Just this circle. And those huge new residence halls they built." I pointed to the buildings in the distance. "Hideous, right?"

"But you still love it here, don't you." He didn't phrase it like a question. He knew I loved it.

"Of course. Coming to this college was the best decision of my life. It led me to you."

He cupped my cheek in his hand. "How much would it upset you to know that some of our donation probably helped pay for those huge hideous buildings."

"A travesty."

He laughed. "And the hospital. That wasn't a travesty."

"No. That was a life saver."

"The personal attention we got at the hospital was impressive," said James. "I don't want to know how much money you donated, but do we practically own that hospital because of all the donations we've made?"

"Probably. But if we ever have any health problems, we know where to come."

His hand slid down the side of my neck in the most distracting way. But the way he was staring at me made it impossible for me to think about anything else.

"Or maybe we should just stay," he said.

"Stay." I stared into his eyes. "In Newark?"

"I can't remember the last time I saw you this happy, Penny. I want to see you smile as much every day as you have in the past few days."

"I smile plenty."

"You haven't smiled plenty. You've been upset in New York. You think I didn't notice you crying after opening the mail? And I've never heard laughter flowing out of your office while you work. You haven't been happy. And somewhere along the way you forgot that I've always seen you, Penny."

I moved a fraction of an inch closer to him. "Are you not happy in New York?"

"Not if you aren't."

I bit the inside of my lip as I stared into his eyes. "The city is our home."

"But it doesn't have to be. We can move anywhere you want."

I shook my head. "I love our apartment. And all our friends are right there."

"All I'm concerned about is your happiness."

"I'm happy in the city."

He shook his head. "I've never seen you climb random statues in Central Park with a huge smile on your face. And I can't remember the last time where we ate so much pizza that our stomachs hurt. Or watched a romantic comedy curled up on the couch together. Or took the time to take a walk just the two of us. Penny. I don't want to go back if your smiles are going to disappear again."

I swallowed hard. Maybe somewhere along the way I had forgotten that he saw me. For what I really was. What I was really thinking. Was I unhappy in New York?

"I think we should stay," he said.

"I don't really understand where this is coming from. We've done nothing but talk about bringing Liam home. Home is in New York. We're leaving in less than an hour."

"But we don't have to. We can stay here. Scarlett can come join us down here."

"Your old apartment is a bachelor pad. It's not home."

"If we brought all our stuff here it would feel like home. I don't want to go back. I don't want to risk losing you."

"Why would you lose me if we went back?"

He shook his head. "Everyone thought...I didn't want to believe it. I told myself it couldn't be true. But it's been eating me alive. You remember the day you went into labor now. I wasn't there. And after I found the note you left...I have to know. Did you try to take your own life? It's been in the back of my mind. And it won't go away. Penny, I need to know. I'll do anything to make you happy and it kills me that..."

"No." I grabbed both sides of his face. "Never." I blinked away the tears in my eyes. "I was worried that something might happen to me. Because of my heart. I wanted to add that letter to the will so that you'd have something to hold on to. Or..." I shook my head. "A push in the right direction of letting me go. I just wanted you to keep our family whole. And happy."

"I'm not whole or happy without you."

"Well good, because I'm not going anywhere. And I'm sorry if I've seemed upset the last year or so. I mean…getting rejection letters has been hard. But you just got me a publishing deal. So I don't really have to worry about that anymore."

"A publishing deal that you're not going to accept. Because it's not what you want."

"It *is* what I want. It's everything I wanted. Not exactly the way I wanted it, no."

"I'm so sorry, Penny."

"It's fine. Besides, it's too late now." I shook my head. "I'll never really know if I had what it took now. But it is what I wanted. And you helped me get it."

"Of course you'll know. You turn down the offer I got you and keep trying."

"Yeah but…literary agents talk. She probably pitched it to more than one publishing house. Everyone will already know that my pen name is actually me."

"No. She worked for an imprint in London. She wouldn't have pitched the idea to anyone else because then another publishing house could have reached out to you to offer you a better deal and cut her out. Besides, she met with me, not you. She doesn't have rights to your story. We didn't sign any paperwork with her. And I never mentioned your pen name. That was for you to hash out with her on your own."

"No one knows my pen name?"

"Or your story. She only read the first few chapters."

"*Our* story. It's our story, James. Not just mine."

"Then let's do this our way. On our own. Self-publish it, Penny."

"I don't know anything about self-publishing."

"Me either. Isn't that half the fun? Besides, a publisher will want to change it. And I don't want you to change one word."

"You really liked it?"

"I loved it." He leaned down and kissed me. "You were meant to do this."

He wasn't trying to help me with his last name or money. He was offering to help me research how to be an indie author. How to create a new business. "I thought I could do this all on my own. But I don't want to. I want to do it with you." I wanted to do everything with him. "But don't get any ideas on Hunter Publishing House or anything else like that. All of this has to be anonymous."

"What, you think I can't be a well behaved Mr. Smoak?" He backed away from me slowly with his eyebrow raised.

"Mr. Smoak. I scrunched my nose up. Stick with Professor Hunter."

He laughed as he hopped up onto the statue. "Now let's see if we can get this echo thing going." He held out his hand for me.

I grabbed it and climbed back up on the statue with him. But we didn't clap. Instead, he pulled me in for a kiss. Right in the middle of campus. And I savored the moment. It was something we'd never been able to do when we first met. Our relationship had been a secret. But he wasn't a professor anymore. And I wasn't a student. We had escaped to New York so we could be ourselves. But he was right, we could move here now and be happy. I just wasn't sure if that's what I wanted.

I pulled away from his kiss. "Rehoboth."

He smiled down at me. "What about it?"

"I want to stay in New York. But we should look into getting a beach house in Rehoboth. Where we can come whenever we need a break from the chaos of the city. It would be perfect with the kids. I loved going to the beach when I was little with my parents. Liam and Scarlett will love it too. And I know you're relaxed at the beach, so if we get away more often..."

"Done. You don't have to sell me on the idea. I think it's great. We can look at properties as soon as you want."

"And we can always stop here on the way down to the beach. Make sure our kids know how important this university is to our family. We can annoyingly point out all the silly changes they make. And talk about the good old days. It'll be perfect."

"Hmm. Perfect." He stared at me like I was the perfect one. Like nothing else in the world mattered to him. We stood in the middle of the statue for a long time, just being happy. Being us. "Let's take our son home," he finally said, breaking the spell.

I felt tears welling in my eyes. Because it wasn't just me who he thought was perfect anymore. He loved his children just as much as he loved me. And *that* was perfect.

He jumped off the statue and pulled me down into his arms. My feet stayed suspended in air as he held me tightly in his embrace.

I had never felt so full. I had come to Newark scared of losing the two men in my life. But I was keeping both of them. Liam was healthy now. And James was too. There was no alternate ending to our story. It had to be a happily ever after.

CHAPTER 21

3 Months Later - Saturday - *Penny*

The seagulls cawed as I walked through the sand. But the sound was mostly drowned out by my family's laughter.

"Welcome to our little slice of paradise," I whispered to Liam as I showed him the ocean for the first time. We had finally found a beach house that was big enough to accommodate our extended family. And this weekend everyone was here to celebrate our new home away from home.

"Most people think paradise has more palm trees. But this is paradise to me too," Melissa said as she stared at the ocean with us.

I glanced down at her stomach. She was finally starting to show. She and Josh had originally planned their trip to help me out while Liam was born. But they also had news of their own that they hadn't shared because of all the chaos. She was pregnant. A wonderful, unexpected surprise for her and Josh. But she was so excited.

"No bikini today?" I asked with a smile. "I swore I wore a bikini the whole time I was pregnant with Scar."

"No. No bikini and no wedding dress until after this little girl is born." She put her hand on her stomach, her engagement ring shining in the sun. "Besides, moving back to New York has been stressful enough. I can't even think about planning anything else."

"It's good to have you back. Even though I had to settle for us being neighbors instead of roomies."

She laughed. "It's crazy how much we've grown up. I mean, who would have guessed we'd be here?"

"I always knew you'd end up with Josh. You guys are perfect together."

"She just needed some time to be convinced," Josh said as he wrapped his arms around her waist and placed a kiss on the side of her neck.

I left them alone as he tried to pull her into the water.

"One day you're going to fall in love," I whispered to Liam. "Way, way in the future. Like Melissa and Josh." I looked up the beach where Mason and Bee were sitting in beach chairs. Bee was waving around sunscreen, probably trying to convince him that he wasn't immune to sunburn just because he was naturally tan. "And Mason and Bee." I bounced Liam on my hip. Tyler and Hailey had wrangled the kids together to build a sandcastle that did not look like it was going to stand up for very long. "And Tyler and Hails." Jen and Ian were up on the boardwalk, staring at the chaos we had unleashed on the beach. "And Jen and Ian." Matt was holding little R.J. in his arms while Rob and Daphne were jumping waves. "Like Rob and Daphne. And Matt...well, I'm sure he'll find someone soon. I'm going to help him."

Liam wiggled in my arms.

"What? I'm a good matchmaker."

He blinked up at me.

"I helped Mason learn that not all girls are lame salad eating divas. And I pushed Tyler away. If I hadn't, he'd never have met Hailey. Plus I kinda accidentally broke up Melissa and Tyler, which sent her back in the arms of Josh in a weird, roundabout way. I encouraged Ian to ask Jen out. And Rob was at James' bachelor party when he started things with Daphne. I feel like that counts too."

He blinked again.

"Fine, technically I've never done any real matchmaking." I sat down in the sand, balancing Liam on my lap. "But that doesn't mean I'll be bad at it. Look at me and your father. That's true love. If anyone knows what the real deal is, it's me. One day, I hope you find love that strong."

"Are you already hoping that Liam's falling in love?" James asked as he walked up to us. "He's only 4 months old."

"No, I'm simply hoping he finds a love as great as ours. And the beach is a great place to fall in love. Don't you think?"

James laughed and sat down beside me. "The only little girls here are his sister and his cousin. So no, I don't think he's going to find love here right now."

"Well, Melissa is having a little girl."

He kissed the side of my forehead. "Let him live his life, Penny."

"I'm not going to interfere in his love life. I promise. Mostly. Okay, fine. I might interfere a little."

He laughed and wrapped his arm around me. We looked out at the ocean in silence, watching the waves splash against the shore.

"I love it here," I said. "Thank you. For all of this. Having everyone here…it's amazing. Are your parents still coming down tomorrow? I think my mom is excited to try to bond with your mother again."

James laughed. "Yeah, they'll be here. Fun tonight and then the parents are arriving in the morning."

"We're parents too." I gently nudged his side.

He wrapped his arm around me, pulling Liam and me close to his chest. "Are you saying we're old and boring now?"

"No. I don't think I could ever describe us as boring. Just old."

"You're not even thirty yet."

"Yeah. But you're well past it."

He laughed. "Touché."

"I'll love you when you're old and gray," I said. I tilted my face up so I could kiss the scruff along his jaw line. "I think I could sit right here until I was old and gray. This is perfect."

"The kiddos certainly love it." We watched as Axel splashed Scarlett and Sophie with water. Both girls screamed at the top of their lungs.

"Our family is perfect." I lifted my head off his shoulder so I could see James' face. "It's the perfect size. I know I was upset when I found out I couldn't have any more kids. But I think...I think this is perfect." I looked down at Liam on my lap. I couldn't possibly ask for more.

"I think so too." James reached over and patted the front of Liam's onesie. "I have everything I'll ever want right here." He looked up at me with a smile on his face. "You know, a few months ago, when you were still trying to remember our family, you fell asleep in my arms while you were talking about how love isn't about light and dark or whirlwinds of color. You said that this right here was love. What we share. What all of us share." He looked back down at our son. Our little miracle breathing easily on his own. "I never told you how much I agree. Love can't really be defined. It isn't a balance of light and darkness or a whirlwind of color. It's a feeling. This feeling." He leaned down and placed a gentle kiss against my lips.

"Daddy! Mommy!" Scarlett ran over and collapsed in front of us in the sand. She rolled around, making herself look like a sugar covered doughnut.

I laughed. "Are you having fun, Scar?"

She stopped rolling. "Yes!" She stood up and launched her sandy self into James' arms.

He kissed the top of her head and smiled over at me.

I didn't remember talking about the definition of love before falling asleep a few months ago. But hearing him say it today brought tears to my eyes. It was like he finally realized that he wasn't some dark cloud in my life. He had finally put his demons at bay. He finally believed that we were made to be together just as much as I had always believed it. And he was right. Nothing in the world mattered but this right here. This feeling when we were together and surrounded by our family. No definition was needed. We lived and breathed it. Love.

PROFESSOR HUNTER

Want to know what Professor Hunter was thinking when he first met Penny?

Find out in *Professor Hunter - Temptation* from James' point-of-view!

To get your free copy of *Professor Hunter*, go to:

www.ivysmoak.com/til-hb

WHAT'S NEXT?

James and Penny got their happy ending, but Matt is still single. Will he find love?

His story begins all the way back in high school...which means you get to see James when he was young. And Rob! And even Isabella.

Read Matt's story: *Empire High Untouchables*...available now!

A NOTE FROM IVY

I was inspired to write a superhero story because I've always loved shows like Arrow and The Flash. And who doesn't love a sexy superhero? There's just something about that mask…

But this story was always more than just sexy superheroes to me. I put my heart and soul into Summer Brooks. I channeled every bad thing that's happened to me and became an emotional wreck while writing this novel. I don't think I've ever cried so hard while writing a character. And I hope that emotion showed in these words. I hope that you cried with me and loved with me.

Ivy Smoak
Wilmington, DE
www.ivysmoak.com

Recommend *This Is Love* for your next book club!

Book club questions available at:
www.ivysmoak.com/bookclub

Printed in the USA
CPSIA information can be obtained
at www.ICGtesting.com
LVHW091041290923
759460LV00010B/154/J

9 781942 381136